BARBAF

Maddie's mate is returning soon, and she wants to make his homecoming a special one. Pregnant Josie wants to seduce her mate all over again. The solution for both of them? A Valentine's Day celebration, ice planet style. There'll be kisses, scanty outfits, and a pair of reunions you won't forget.

Come and revisit two of your favorite couples from the original *Ice Planet Barbarians* series!

BARBARIAN'S VALENTINE

AN ICE PLANET BARBARIANS SLICE OF LIFE

RUBY DIXON

ICE PLANET BARBARIANS - BOOK 19

Copyright © 2019 by Ruby Dixon

All rights reserved.

No part of this book may be reproduced in any form or by any electronic or mechanical means, including information storage and retrieval systems, without written permission from the author, except for the use of brief quotations in a book review.

Cover Photo - Shutterstock

Cover Design - Kati Wilde

Edits - Aquila Editing

❦ Created with Vellum

1

MADDIE

"It's another clear day, baby boo. You know what this means?" I return inside my hut, practically singing the words out, I'm so happy.

My son Masan looks up from where he's playing with his pet bird. He's still in his jammies, and the damn thing's on his lap as he gently feeds her chewed up bits of seed. But his little face lights up when he hears my announcement. "Papa's coming home soon?"

"Yup!" I tell him happily. It's the brutal season, and Hassen's been over at the beach for the last few months, helping teach the newcomers how to take care of themselves and survive. A few rounds of people have returned, including our chief, but my mate is still there. I know he's helping out because he's needed and Hassen's a good person at heart. He loves to help out.

But this Mama Bear is ready for Papa Bear to get his ass home because Mama Bear is SUPER horny and needs to get laid. I think of my delicious mate, all tall and thick and gorgeous, and my girl parts tingle with need. If he isn't coming home soon, I'm going to him on the next round, because I am not a woman designed for celibacy. It sucks, and I never thought I would need—or miss—a man nearly as much as I miss my Hassen. He's been gone before, but never quite so long, and I've moved past the whole "I'm independent and fine" to "weeping into my pillow at night."

At least I have his son to keep me occupied. I move to Masan's side and plant a kiss on my son's brow, then push his messy hair out of his eyes. He's inherited his father's gorgeous thick black hair, but he's also inherited my flyaways and he always looks a bit untidy. "How's your bird?"

"She's getting fat," he tells me proudly, beaming up at me. "And she slept with me last night."

I wrinkle my nose at the thought. "Did she, now?"

He nods and scoops up the damn thing, utterly pleased. "Millicent's so smart."

"So I guess she's not gonna fly away anytime soon, huh?" When he gives me a hurt look, I just press another kiss to his brow. "I'm teasing you, Masan. You can keep her for as long as you like, but the moment she starts building a nest, she is an outdoor bird, do you hear me?" Because dirtbeaks are gross. They build their nests with just about the only "soil" they can reach given the thick layer of snow covering the ground at all times—that means dvisti dung chips. Which, yeah, no. I'm trying to be an understanding mama, but I draw the line at a poop nest in my house.

Sometimes I wish that Masan hadn't been the kid to find the baby dirtbeak that had fallen out of its nest on one of the egg runs. But my son loves animals, and he's utterly fascinated with

Farli's Chompy and Kate's kitten, so I wasn't entirely surprised that he brought the thing home. It keeps him busy while his father's away, so I don't mind it as much as I should. The darn thing was so scrawny and ugly, all sharp edges and flat, slimy-looking dark feathers that it seemed positively hideous and evil looking, so I'd suggested the name Maleficent.

My sweet boy couldn't remember the name Maleficent and it somehow ended up as "Millicent" instead. I guess it fits the poor bird, considering she's really filled out in the last few weeks. He's been diligent about feeding her and taking care of her, and he carries her everywhere with him in the cutest little basket. She looks kind of like a tiny indignant cross between a chicken and a toucan now, with dark feathers and a long bill and blinking eyes that watch me far too closely.

I'm not a fan of birds. If it was up to me, Millicent would have gone home with some other kit, but my little Masan is not a tough cookie like his mama. He's a sensitive child, and ever since Millicent arrived, he's stopped crying at night because his papa's gone.

Bless that dumbass bird.

"Do you think Papa will like her?" He looks up at me with hopeful eyes, hugging the bird to his chest as she pecks at his chin.

"I'm sure he will," I reassure my son. "He's going to be so proud of you when he sees what a good job you've done with her." And I love that my little son puffs up so proudly, beaming. For a moment, he looks just like his father and my heart squeezes with loneliness.

God, I want my man home already.

But it's been two days of clear weather, and Veronica and Ashtar promised that they'd fly again in a few weeks, when we had a break in the brutal season storms. It's colder than a penguin's tit right now, but the skies are crystalline blue and that means—hopefully—that Veronica and Ashtar will be flying in for a visit.

And I hope Hassen is hitching a ride, or I'm going to kill him.

I can't help but get excited as I move around the hut, making breakfast for my son (and his bird). I cook and straighten up the small kitchen area as I do, inwardly wincing at how I've let the housekeeping slide while my husband wasn't home. Okay, not that I've ever been a great housekeeper, but now that he's coming home, I want to wow him, and a messy kitchen is not the way to do it.

Then again, will he care about the kitchen? We won't be leaving the furs for days.

"You're giggling, Mama. What's so funny?" Masan asks.

I clear my throat and plate up some scrambled eggs for him. "Just excited about Papa coming home, baby boo. Thinking about all the things I need to get done between now and then."

And oh, there is gonna be a lot to get done. I think of how I want to greet Hassen, and idea after delicious, sexy idea unfurls in my mind. I'm thinking I find a babysitter for Masan and Millicent, put on some sexy clothing, and go to town on my gorgeous husband.

"You're giggling again, Mama."

"So I am. Eat your eggs."

He feeds Millicent her nut mash and we eat our eggs, and then I help my son bundle up for the cold weather. He gets his basket and declares that he's going to take Millicent out to play. That's fine with me, because if he has her with him, I don't have to watch over her and make sure she doesn't poop inside the house. Is this what moms with new puppies feel like, I wonder? Except they're probably not picking stray feathers out of everything in sight. "I'm going to go visit Aunt Lila and bring her food," I tell him as I tug another layer over his head. "You stay in the village, okay? Don't go farther out than Bek and Elly's hut."

Masan makes an exasperated sound. "But Joden wants to get a dirtbeak of his own. He's gonna go shake nests and see if he can get a baby out so he can have his own Millicent."

"Uh, no, you are not doing that," I tell him. "You tell Joden if I hear he's doing that I'm going to get his papa. You stay in the village, and play with Millicent, and no visiting the other dirtbeaks, understand?"

Masan's lower lip sticks out, but he nods. We put his little gloves on and then I grab a fur cloak and bundle up before picking up the bowl of food I've got prepared. It's a lot of work to just go down the "street," but it's nasty-cold this time of year. Once we're outside, the frostiness hits your face like a wall, but my son doesn't notice it. With his bird basket, he skips down the walk, heading right for Josie's hut where a few of the kits are playing outside already. I watch for a moment as he races up to a heavily bundled Joden and says something. Joden nods and produces a small stick, and then they set Millicent gently down on the ground and wave it in front of her face.

Are...they going to try to teach a dirtbeak to fetch a stick? That's cute. Kinda pointless, but cute. I watch a moment longer to make sure that they're behaving and then head next door to Lila's hut. The screen's on the front, but I can hear someone moving around inside and they have a fire going, so they're up. I scratch at the screen.

Rokan appears in the doorway a moment later, the baby in his arms. He puts a finger to his lips, indicating quiet, and invites me in.

I step inside, and I see my sister's still in bed, sleeping. There are dark circles under her eyes and I wince in sympathy. "Lolo still not sleeping through the night?" I whisper.

Rokan pats the baby's back, rocking her in a gentle motion as she sleeps. "She does not feed as easily as Rollan did. Last night she wanted to nurse every handful of minutes. My Li-lah did not get much sleep, so I am letting her rest until Lo-lo needs to nurse again."

I squeeze his arm sympathetically. He's a good man and very protective of my sister, which I approve of. Little newborn Lola—who we call Lolo more than anything—has been the screamiest, unhappiest baby, and it's wearing Lila out, so I'm glad Rokan's home to be with her. We've done this a few mornings now, quietly puttering around to try and let Lila get some sleep. I move to the kitchen area, spoon some of the food into a cooking pouch to warm it, and then set it on the tripod over the fire to heat up. As Rokan continues to rock the sleeping baby, I cross the hut and peer into Rollan's sleeping corner. He's sitting up, quietly waiting, and beams at me. What a great kid, my nephew.

"Let's get you dressed," I whisper, "and get some breakfast into you so you can play outside. The boys are trying to teach Millicent how to fetch a stick."

His face lights up, and within a space of a few minutes, he's layered up and ready to go outside. I snag him and make him eat breakfast first, and then send him on his way once he's done, his chipmunk cheeks still full of eggs as he races out to meet the others.

That done, I straighten up my sister's house as quietly as I can, mindful of the fact that she's sleeping and the baby is, too. I pick up clothes and tidy up her tiny kitchen, and then glance over at Rokan. The dad looks almost as tired as my sister, but he continues to sway back and forth, over and over, his big hand cradling Lolo's tiny back.

"You need anything?" I ask quietly. "Want me to babysit for a few hours?"

Rokan gives me a tired smile and shakes his head. "I am weary, but there is no place I would rather be than here holding my daughter and watching over my mate."

I smile at that.

He rubs his hand up Lolo's little back and then gives me a curious look. "Two days of good weather, is it not?"

"It is," I say, and practically dance with excitement. "Is Hassen coming home? Does your 'knowing' tell you anything?" Rokan's got this weird psychic ability to know things before anyone else does, and he's never wrong.

"Very soon," he agrees. "Hassen will be excited to see you. He has told everyone at the Icehome camp about you."

"Of course he has. I'm awesome." But it feels good to know that my gorgeous husband has been gushing about me to other women. Suck on that, ladies. He's mine. "I'm trying to think of a way for us to celebrate when he gets home."

"I am sure there will be a celebration."

Yeah, but I'm trying to think of ways for me to privately celebrate with my man, not with the tribe. "I was thinking a sitter so we could have some alone time but...I don't think Lila's up for the job." I look over at my sleeping sister. She's making me tired just looking at her and I would never ask while she's got a fussy newborn. "Any ideas?"

"Perhaps Summer and Warrek, then? It might be a good idea for Rollan to spend time with Warrek. Give my mate some time to relax and Warrek has many things he can teach."

"Oh, that's a good idea. We can pose it as a cousins' sleepover." My son will never be the wiser that his parents really just want to get ultra-freaky for a few hours. "You're a genius."

Lolo stirs, a little whimper in the back of her throat. We both freeze, but she shoves one little three-fingered hand into her mouth and sucks on it, going back to sleep against her father's chest.

Rokan breathes a sigh of relief.

I point at the door and use sign language instead. *I'm going to go*, I tell him. *I'll check with Warrek. If you need anything, just say.*

He gives me a thumbs up and sways with the baby once more, and I ease my way out of their hut, tiptoeing.

I pause to check on the boys for a few minutes, watching them play. It looks like the stick game has turned into a round of chase, and Millicent follows behind Masan's heels, waddling as fast as her plumed little bird feet will take her as he chases Rollan. At least they're all still in the village and behaving, as far as I can tell. Joden's a good kid, but he's also a kid with a lot of ideas, and not all of them good ones.

When they run close, I wave them over and fix Masan's hat for him. "You boys come to my hut for lunch, okay? Rollan's mommy is sleeping." I look around and notice that Joden isn't with them anymore. "Where's Joden?"

"His papa came and got him," Masan tells me, breathless. "They are going herb hunting because his mommy has a bad tummy. Can we go herb hunting, Mama?"

Plants? Yick. I'm still not very good at telling them apart. "Maybe later. Right now, Mama's going to go talk to Summer and Warrek, and then I'm going to make an extra-special dinner to take over to Auntie Lila and Uncle Rokan's house." I beam at them. "Won't that be yummy? We can even make not-cookies with some cooked hraku seeds I've been saving."

"Not-cookies!" they both cry, dancing with excitement.

"Yup, not-cookies," I agree, since they're not like the cookies I remember but mostly a hash-up of nutty crap baked over a fire, but the kids love them as a special treat. "But you have to play outside for a while first, OK? Stay here and I'm going to go visit Summer and Warrek. I'll be back."

I wipe snotty noses, fix clothes, and then send them on their way. A few of the other kits have come out to play, and I see the cute blonde pigtails of the twins, along with the wild curls of Georgie's girls. It's not a class day and I worry there's going to be no parent watching over them, but Nora steps out a moment later and waves at me, then sits on the stone bench in front of her hut, and Old Drenol's sitting on the bench in front of his hut, with Lukti at his side. That's good enough for adult supervision for now, which means I can slip over to Summer and Warrek's hut.

I head down the path, toward "Newlywed Lane" as we like to joke. All of the newly mated couples have taken up houses near the back of the settlement for privacy reasons, and it makes me sigh, thinking how much fun it was to be newly mated with nothing to do all day but fuck like bunnies. Not that I'd trade Masan for anything. I love that boy so fiercely it makes me hurt inside. But I'm also envious of the bright, new joy I see on Harrec and Kate's faces when they look at each other. Or Bek and Elly, who seem to be in a world all their own.

My man really needs to come back. Maybe we'll resonate a

second time like Kira and Aehako did, and spark the new, fresh magic of a mating all over again. I touch my stomach, thinking about that. A second baby. I like the idea...but I also think about how tired Lila is. Sleepless nights trying to comfort a fussy baby, breastfeeding that made my already big tits utterly enormous and painful, and having no free time to myself because there was another person entirely dependent on me. Hassen helped, of course, but he also had to do a lot of hunting, and some nights it was just me and a cranky baby. It's kind of nice now that Masan is older and turning into his own person instead of just a needy little mouth...but then I think of sweet baby Lolo, and how amazing resonating was.

And how fucking intense the sex was.

Kinda a toss-up. I guess I'd be happy either way, really.

It's all moot if my mate doesn't come home, anyhow. But I'm going to think positive. Rokan said some encouraging things and the weather is still nice, and so I head over to Summer and Warrek's hut and scratch cheerfully on their door.

Immediately, I hear a lot of scrambling inside. "Coming!" Summer yelps. "Uh, just a minute!"

I smirk to myself, because I recognize that distracted tone of voice. Someone just got caught having sex.

"Coming!" she calls again.

"Or not," I mutter under my breath, delighted at my own pun.

A moment later, Summer comes to the door and pulls it aside. She's flushed, her smooth black hair disheveled. Her shoulders are bare and she clutches a fur to her breasts to hide her nudity. "Oh, hi Maddie. We weren't expecting someone to come by."

"That's the shortest sentence you've ever said to me," I point out, grinning. "Can I come in?"

"No," she blurts immediately, and then bites her lip, looking embarrassed. "We were in the middle of, ah, a game. And you'd see a lot more than you'd really want to see if you come in, not that I'm ashamed of anything Warrek has, but you know…" Her voice trails off and she closes her eyes as the tall, lean hunter comes up behind her and loops an arm around her shoulder, hugging her back against him. I'm pretty sure he's buck-ass nekkid, as I can't see a stitch of clothing on him from where I'm standing. He presses a kiss to the top of his mate's head and just gives me a very lazy, satisfied smile.

"So I can't come in? What, are all the sex toys out?" I cross my arms, amused.

Summer makes a horrified squeaking sound, but Warrek just grins. "Um, no, we were playing, ah…strip chess." Summer wrinkles her nose. "That's all."

"That's a thing?" Strip chess might be the nerdiest thing I've ever heard. I eye her. "Looks like you're both losing."

She gives a breathless giggle and leans back against him and looks so happy that I ache for my Hassen. "We like to try out different strategies."

"Is that what we're calling it?" I shrug. "Look, you don't have to explain to me. I'm sure everyone in the camp has heard me and Hassen hooking up." And half of them have caught us, since we sorta have a thing for doing it in public places where we might get caught. "I need a favor, though. Rokan says that Hassen might be coming home soon and I want to have some alone time with him. I wanted to see if you and Warrek could watch Masan—and possibly Rollan to give Lila a break—for a night or two. Feel free to say no—"

"Yes," Warrek says simply. He presses another kiss to Summer's head.

"Oh? Okay, cool."

"Sure, bring them over." Summer hugs the arm he has around her shoulders, practically losing the fur she's wearing. She looks so stinking happy it's cute, and I'm jealous. "We'll come up with something for them to do."

"You're sure?"

"Of course. Your man's coming home...are you going to surprise him? Do something special?"

Something special? I was thinking about flinging him to the furs and just banging him for a day straight, but I do like the idea of something special. "I'm not really sure Hassen would like a surprise party. The only surprises he really likes are sexy, private ones."

She laughs. "So make it a sexy, private party. Or celebrate a personal holiday."

"No—Poison already passed."

"Val-en-time," Warrek says, rubbing his thumb on Summer's naked shoulder.

"Oh, yes! You guys should do a Valentine's Day thing. Me and Warrek are going to have our own celebration." And she blushes again, while Warrek just looks like a cat that ate the cream. "Make some sweets, give each other gifts, celebrate your love..."

"Play some strip chess?" I add sweetly.

She giggles. "Or that."

Valentine's Day. The more I roll the idea around in my head, the more I think it's perfect. I'm getting pretty good at sewing, and I have some boning I was going to use for a hood...but I could make a sexy corset instead. Isn't that what Valentine's Day is all about? Corsets and roses and sexy things? "I'm totally stealing that idea," I say.

"It's a holiday. You can't steal it." Summer smiles. "Just let us know when you need us to watch the boys and we'll be ready."

"Not today," Warrek says, and that's rather chatty of him. He gives me a wicked grin and scoops his mate into his arms. "I'm winning."

"Not today," I agree, and as he takes his giggling mate back into the depths of their hut, I shut their door for them and head back to watch the kids.

Lingerie. Sweets. A sexy celebration. Valentine's Day, barbarian style.

I'm loving the idea.

2

HAEDEN

*I*t is a good thing I am not hunting this day, because my small son has not yet remembered that the best way to find animals is silence.

"Is that the flower we need, Papa?" At my side, Joden points at the closest bush.

"No."

"That one?" He points at the bush next to it.

"Still no."

"What about that one?"

"Joden, we would not walk past it if we needed it," I explain patiently.

"Then maybe that one?" He points ahead of us, at a few ice-crusted bushes hiding in the shadow of a cliff.

I bite back a sigh. I have already told him twice that we are looking for the leaves of a soothing plant, which grows near the banks of the hot streams and has tiny bright red flowers. But I know my son is curious and determined to be helpful, so I endure his talking. Most of the time, I enjoy his nonsense chatter because it makes me imagine it is how Jo-see was as a kit. Today, though, it is difficult to appreciate. My mate had a sleepless night, as this kit is more difficult for her to carry, and when she suffers, I suffer. Now I am tired and must watch my son, who has boundless amounts of energy.

But I remain calm, because it is my son. We have talked in circles a hundred times before and will do it a hundred times again. "What plant are we looking for, my son?" I ask, reminding him. "Which one did Mommy say she wanted?"

"Soothing plant," he chirps up at me, holding my hand as we walk the trail. "Because the baby in her tummy is mad."

Close enough. "That is right."

"Is that why Mommy's tummy has those angry red lines on it?"

"Your mother says they are called 'stretch marks' in her world and it happens when a mama's stomach gets big with her kit."

"Mommy sure has a lot of them," he says cheerfully. "That baby must be really angry."

"She is growing a kit. That is all." I have told him before that his mother has had lines on her belly ever since he was born, and I find them just as beautiful now as I did then. But Joden is young and tends to only remember that which interests him. So I simply say, "It is part of making a kit."

"Why do we need more kits?" He looks up at me. "You have a boy and a girl now. Why do we need more?"

"Because we resonated again," I tell him. "The khui has chosen for you to have more brothers or sisters."

"Do you want more of them?"

I think. Having kits is an endless amount of work, much more than I ever thought imaginable. One finally learns not to soil his wraps and then a new one comes along. One starts sleeping through the night...and the other wets the bed. It is always something, and Jo-see and I have not had a good night's sleep since Joden's arrival. It is work, true, but there are smiles and sweet laughter, and small hands that clutch at yours as if you will save them from the world, and...yes, I want more kits. My Jo-see has always wanted as many as she can imagine, and I like that idea very much. "Mommy wants more," I say, hoping that putting the emphasis on Jo-see will turn the questions back to our task at hand.

"What about you?"

"I want what your mother wants." On this, we are very much agreed.

"Are you sure?" Joden asks me, openly skeptical. "You and Mommy haven't tickled lately."

"Tickled?" My mouth twitches.

"Yes. I've seen you having tickle fights at night."

"Mmm." Tickling. I shall have to tell Jo-see what he said. The thought is amusing. "Your mama is too tired to tickle lately," I tell him. Joha is toddling around now, which means that she puts everything in her mouth. The other day, she ate one of Teef-ah-nee's plants and vomited for two days straight. It was very hard on Jo-see and me both, and my mate has hovered over her ever since. That, plus the kit in her stomach, have drained her and she is tired. Much too tired for her mate to fumble at her and demand a mating, so I have left her alone. We have all the time in the world to touch, and I am content to hold her close and know she is safe.

"Do you and Mommy only tickle when there's a baby to be made?"

I think of my mate, of the tired rings under her eyes. My poor Josee. I want to take all of the cares in the world from her shoulders and put them onto mine. "You have to mate when your khui tells you," I say to him, distracted. "Look. We are almost at the stream. Do you remember what the soothing plant looks like?"

Joden skips ahead, releasing my hand. "It's brown, right?"

"Not brown." With a sigh, I chase after him before he can get into trouble.

3

JOSIE

"Is the tea helping, Mommy? Papa said the tea would make your stomach all better." Joden sits next to me by the fire. "He said it would make the baby in your tummy less mad."

"That is not what I said," Haeden corrects, putting more fuel on the fire. He passes by me as he bustles around our small hut, his hand landing atop my head and stroking my hair before moving on. That small caress makes me smile into my cup and somehow the day feels just a little better.

Then the baby in my stomach kicks my bladder and I groan. The last two pregnancies were so easy. This one just feels like the kit is sitting all wrong every day, and if my stomach isn't hurting, I have to pee or I'm sleeping all the time. Maylak assures me it's normal, and even Georgie's having a hell of a pregnancy, so I guess I can't complain, but it's hard and I'm not good at being sick.

"Looks like baby's still mad," Joden announces. He leans over and whispers to my stomach. "Calm down in there!"

"No, Joha," Haeden says before I can respond. He bounds across the room and pulls our toddling daughter into his arms. "Spit it out."

"No!" she says around a mouthful of seeds.

He puts his hand out and her face scrunches up as if she's going to cry, and then she slowly leans forward and lets them dribble out of her mouth, filling his palm with slobber and half-chewed seeds.

I get to my feet. "Oh no. Not the holiday decorations again. I thought we put those away?" Joha loves to try and eat the seeds because they're painted bright, pretty colors, but she doesn't understand that we painted them instead of eating them precisely because they taste so terrible.

"I got it out, Mommy," Joden says, picking up his favorite ball and toying with one of the stitches on it. "We needed a string for Millicent to chase and I thought she might like the colors."

Haeden casts me a look and shakes his head. "Joden, we have talked about this. Remember?"

"I know. Joha puts everything in her mouth so we gotta hide it all." He rolls his eyes as if he's fourteen instead of four.

"I should have realized," I murmur, getting to my feet. As I do, I wince, everything in me aching. I put a hand under my belly—which seems to be enormous already and I still have a ton of time left to go. I look around the hut. It's a disaster, because Joden is a walking tornado of mess. With a toddler, too? And me pregnant with number three? The place always seems to be cluttered and messy, and I feel guilty. "I'll clean up—"

"No, Jo-see." Haeden wipes the last of half-chewed seeds off of Joha's mouth and then cleans his hand off on one of the small leather squares I use as "kitchen towels." "You are tired. Your feet are swollen. You sit down and rest."

"But you were going to check your traps since the weather's nice," I protest, even though lying down does sound fantastic right about now. It's early, but I'm still tired. I'm always tired.

"They can wait." He tucks Joha under his arm and grabs one of the big, carved bone bowls that he gave me last No-Poison Day as a gift. "I will take the kits and we will see what Stay-see is cooking at the main fire today. You can just relax."

I bite my lip, because it sounds like heaven. I know he's tired too, though. The brutal season is hard on the hunters, and Haeden has been putting in extra hunting time because some of the hunters are at Icehome beach. He's come home late several days, and I know he probably wants to rest just as much as I do, not chase after our two crazy kids after having Joden all morning to boot.

"I'm going to stay with Mommy," Joden announces. "Mommy can lie down and I'll help her clean up!" He picks up his ball and trots across the hut to his little bed and the basket for his toys and sets it inside. "See?"

Haeden and I exchange a look. Joden has more energy than three people combined, but if he thinks he's helping, it could keep him busy for a while. "Why don't I keep Joden with me," I say. "And you take Joha."

He frowns and then pulls one of his braids out of our daughter's slobbery mouth. "If you are certain..."

"It's fine," I say brightly. "We'll play clean up. Won't that be fun, Joden?"

"Really fun, Mommy!" He grabs another one of his toys and begins to singsong our "clean up" chant. "Clean up, clean up, everything has a special place! Clean up, clean up, puts a smile right on my face!"

Haeden just shakes his head and smiles, then leans in to give me a kiss. "We will be back soon."

I give him a peck and watch as he leaves with Joha, then settle down on the furs and lift up my swollen feet. "Mommy's going to elevate her feet while you do such a good job, Joden, okay?"

"Okay, Mommy!" And he launches into another round of the clean up chant.

My son occupied, I relax and watch him as he moves around the house and picks up things to put them away. Because he's young, a lot of the stuff just ends up in a pile in the middle of the room, but I can't be mad about that. He's trying, and he's happy to help, and it keeps him busy. At his age, that's a blessing.

"Mommy, what's this?"

I jerk awake, rubbing my eyes. I must have dozed off as Joden puttered around. The hut's still a huge mess, and it looks like Joden's gotten out my basket of spare clothes and is now "helping" put them away into the big pile of things in the center of the room. "What, baby?" I sit up, trying to focus on him. "What's what?"

He holds up a leather thong and a small, pale plastic T-shaped item. "What's this thing in your stuff?"

"Oh." I take it from him, studying it with a smile. It's my old IUD, the one I hated so much because I wanted resonance so badly, and then when it fell out and I resonated to Haeden, I thought the world was ending. Now I keep it as a reminder of how amazing life can be, no matter the curveballs it throws your way. "It's Mommy's good luck charm."

"Is it a bone?" He wrinkles his nose at it.

"No, it's something Mommy used to wear back on Earth." I don't tell him where I used to wear it, though. "I don't wear it now, but I keep it because it changed everything. It's the reason me and your papa got together."

"I thought it was because you resonated to have me?" He tilts his head, his small horns cocking.

"That, too."

He sits next to me on the furs. "Maybe you should wear it again so Papa will tickle you more often."

I hold my breath. Having small children means that you shouldn't be surprised by anything that comes out of their mouths, but this one shocks me. "What?"

"Papa says he can't tickle you because you're too tired. And he only tickles you to make more babies, so maybe you should wear that so he'll tickle you again."

It's like a knife in my fragile heart. "He...said that?" I know that Joden just parrots everything he overhears, and it's wrong a lot of the time, but I can't deny that it's been weeks since Haeden and I have had sex. I've been a mess with this pregnancy, and then Joha was sick, and...I try to think of the last time we touched each other more than a quick kiss.

It's been more than weeks. At least a moon, then?

I'm horrified at the realization. Suddenly, I feel bloated and ugly and undesirable. I swallow hard, trying not to get upset. "Papa and Mommy have been busy, honey."

"Papa says he tickles you to make the babies, and that he only wants more cuz you want more."

I feel like vomiting. Haeden wants more children. We've always joked that we want tons of babies. But...maybe the reality isn't what he expected? Maybe he misses the constant sex instead of nappy changes and plucking things out of Joha's mouth? I love sex with him, but...I love our babies, too.

And I'm growing a third one right now.

My hand strays to my stomach and the kit inside there immediately kicks my bladder. I wince and get to my feet. Am I...disappointing him as a wife? Should I be more sexual despite all the babies? Sometimes I feel like I'm doing good to make it through the day and I know Haeden feels the same...but maybe he expects more?

All these things Joden is saying can't be coming out of nowhere, can they? They have to be because of some sort of conversation he had with his father, and that makes my heart hurt. Is Haeden disappointed in me somehow?

A child screams outside, followed by giggles. I can hear them playing, and Joden's head turns with excitement. Suddenly, I just want to be alone. I get to my feet. "That sounds like Anna and Elsa. Why don't you go play with them? Mommy will finish cleaning up."

My son doesn't protest. He immediately races for his fur wraps, and we bundle him up so he can go outside. The moment his hat is pulled over his little horns, he grabs his ball and races outside. I peek out to see who's supervising, smile at Nora and wave, and then retreat back into my house for a nice, long cry.

And I promptly trip over the enormous pile of crap Joden created in the middle of the floor. I manage to catch myself before I fall on my ass, but it just makes my bad mood even worse. I can feel my lip wobbling as I pick up once-folded clean laundry and then just start weeping uncontrollably.

I tell myself that it's just a pregnancy mood. That my gorgeous alien mate still loves his plain little human female and still wants sex with her. That it's not just because of resonance. But when I look down at my swollen feet and equally swollen belly with bright red stretch marks all over it, it's hard to feel sexy and desirable. If I can't imagine anyone having sex with me, how can he want me? All I do is sleep and crap out babies. Maybe life with me isn't what he imagined it would be, and that makes my heart hurt. Is he sick of me? Or maybe he just doesn't want as many babies as we've been having?

That hurts me just as much. I love our growing family. I'm excited for each kit, even if I'm tired and swollen right now and Joha gave me the scare of my life when she ate Tiffany's potency plant, which is basically Viagra and made my poor little girl barf her lungs out, all because I was tired and hadn't watched her as closely as I should have.

Maybe...maybe Haeden thinks I'm a bad mother.

The thought makes me sob even harder.

Someone scratches at the screen over the door. I swipe at my running nose and lumber to my feet. "C-coming." It's probably Nora, here to tell me that Joden just pulled one of Elsa's pigtails or stole Holvek's stuffed toy again. I love my little son, but he's definitely a handful.

To my surprise, Maddie sticks her head in. "Hey, uh, is this a bad time?"

I'm astonished to see her. Maddie and I have always been friendly, but we haven't had many one-on-one visits. I'm usually wrapped up in Haeden and my babies, or I spend my time with Megan or Georgie. Maddie hangs with her sister more than the rest of us, too. "No, no, come in. I was just having a hormonal moment." I give her a wobbly smile.

She ducks into my hut and shoots me an odd look. "You're never hormonal. You're the happiest pregnant lady ever. In fact, you make the rest of us look bad with all the babies you're popping out."

I burst into a new round of tears. Is that all I am to everyone else, then? Just one big baby-making machine?

"Whoa, hey, okay." Maddie puts an arm around my shoulders, gently steering me towards the seating near the fire. "You sit down and tell me what's bothering you, okay? And while you sit, I'm going to straighten up. It always helps Lila feel better when she's overwhelmed with the babies. You want some tea?"

I'm touched at how thoughtful she is. "Tea would be lovely, and you don't have to straighten up. Joden was helping me." I gesture at the enormous pile in the middle of the floor.

"Yeah, I figured. Masan likes to 'help' too." She rolls her eyes and chuckles to herself, then putters around in my kitchen, pulling out ingredients for tea. "Now tell me why we're weeping today."

She's so at ease with herself, so relaxed in her own skin. Maddie's...well, Maddie's really plump. Stacy's solid and says her butt's spreading now that she's had kids, and Nora's always complaining about her figure, but Maddie is easily the biggest girl in the camp. She's also the most confident. She's really gorgeous, with wild blonde hair that always looks tousled and sexy, and she's got these enormous boobs that always look amazing no matter what she wears, and she looks like she's never had an ugly day in her life. It doesn't matter that she's got the biggest hips in the camp, and it's clear that her mate Hassen finds her to be the most gorgeous thing ever.

I'm so envious of her confidence. As she makes tea and moves around my place, straightening up, I find myself confessing my insecurities. That I'm tired and bloated and Joden's words made me worry that I'm not attractive to my mate anymore. That he doesn't want our life or so many kits. That he regrets our family.

That we haven't had sex in over a month.

Maddie doesn't laugh at my fears or tell me I'm being silly or hormonal. When I mention the sex thing she just sighs heavily and nods, pouring herself a cup of tea, too. Then she sits beside me and offers me one. "Girl, I know that feeling. All my girl parts are going to shrivel up and die if I don't get some dick soon."

I sputter-choke on my first sip of tea, then giggle. "That's part of the problem, I think. When I was pregnant with Joha, I wanted sex all the time. Like, ALL the time. But with this baby, I'm just... tired. And achy. Sometimes I want sex, and sometimes I just want a nap. But I don't want Haeden to feel as if he's married to this big gross baby-machine instead of old sex-fiend Josie. You know?" I can feel a new round of tears about to come on.

"Oh, girl," Maddie says, shaking her head. She reaches out and fingers my messy brown braid. "When was the last time you washed your hair? Or undid this braid?"

I shrug. "I make sure the babies are clean."

"This isn't about them, this is about you and feeling sexy. You'll feel good if you look good." She waggles her eyebrows at me. "Hassen's coming home soon and I'm going to surprise him with some sexy lingerie. I'm sending the kids—well, Masan and

Rollan—to Warrek and Summer for a night or two, and I'm going to rock that man's world. That's why I came over. I'm making a sexy leather corset and wanted some white fur to trim it with, and Tiff said you had some extra?" Her eyes gleam with pleasure.

Oh. "Sure, I do. I made Joha the cutest little hood and trimmed it with fur, but there's plenty left over. You can have all of it." I lean in, my belly pressing against my legs as I hold my teacup. "Leather lingerie? Really?"

"Why not? I made a bra and panties out of leather. I can use bones for boning support, and make something sexy instead of just functional. Surprise my man, you know? And if I feel sexy, I know I'll be in the mood that much quicker…not that it takes much to get me in the mood." She grins. "We're going to celebrate a private Valentine's Day."

I touch my braid. Maybe she's right. Maybe I need to dig myself out of this pregnancy rut that I'm in and make myself wildly sexy to seduce my man and remind him how good we are together. That we're more than just resonance partners, we're friends and lovers. "Can I steal that idea?"

"Of course! The more the merrier." She pauses and then gestures. "Well, not in our private Valentine's Day. That's gonna be just me and Hassen. But you know what I mean. We can work on our sexy outfits together. And I'll talk to Summer and Warrek about adding Joden and maybe Joha into the mix. I'm sure they won't mind."

I snort. "Have you met my son?"

She giggles into her tea. "You have a point."

I'm smiling, though. I like this. I like the idea of taking some time alone together, celebrating a holiday, and reconnecting.

And sexy lingerie. That's always a good idea. I feel better already.

Maddie leaves after we talk some strategy over tea, and then I spend the rest of the afternoon watching the kits as they play outside. I sit my leather scrap basket at my side and pick through it while Joden runs around, screaming like a banshee and chasing Holvek and the twins. Haeden returns with food, and then we sit next to each other in the faint sunshine. He works on sharpening bone spearheads while I pick out pieces of fur for my secret creation and Joha plays in her pen nearby. I almost hope Haeden's going to ask me what I'm working on, but he never does. Instead, we talk about small things—the weather, Joha's teething, the fact that Joden doesn't listen in Ariana's classes—and I can't bring myself to ruin an otherwise wonderful afternoon.

After dinner, the kits go to bed and I kiss their sweet little faces as they lie down. Haeden tucks them into their furs and then pulls the divider across the way so the fire doesn't keep them awake.

Then it's just me and Haeden.

I poke at my sewing, fighting back a yawn.

"Tired?" he murmurs, and gives my shoulder an absent caress as he banks the fire. "Let us go to bed as well, then."

Oooh, for sex? Encouraged, I put my sewing away and change into my sleeping tunic. Maybe all my fears were for nothing. He's just been waiting for the right moment.

But when we get under the furs, he's still wearing his pants instead of being naked. Instead of giving me a passionate kiss, he pulls my tunic up and exposes my big belly. He touches it, rubbing his hand gently over the rounded swell, and I can't decide if I'm hurt or pleased. He's an amazing father, and there's no denying he loves the kits...but I don't know what to think.

"Your belly is very big this time," he murmurs to me, fingers tracing along a fresh stretch mark.

Maybe he doesn't realize that telling a very pregnant woman that is a bad call. I've been on the ice planet long enough to know that a lot of things get lost in translation, and human women get upset over things that would never faze a sa-khui woman. Plus, I'm being ultra-sensitive today, which I fully acknowledge.

"What if it's two babies?" I ask, and I can feel myself tensing. "Like Nora's twins?"

Haeden grunts. His hand strokes over the massive bulge of my belly. "Then we will be exhausted and miserable."

That is…not encouraging. There's a teasing note in his voice, but I worry he's trying to mask how he really feels. "What if it's three? That happens on Earth sometimes. In fact, one woman had eight babies at once. Her stomach was freaking enormous."

He looks up at me and his hand goes still across the mountain of my belly. "Why are you worrying so much, Jo-see? This is not our first kit."

I force myself to meet his gaze, to put a smile on my face. "I'm not worrying, just curious. Want to have sex?"

There's something in my voice that alerts him to how I really feel—either that or I have a terrible poker face. He props up on one elbow and stares at me, hard. "Jo-see, what is wrong?"

I twist the edge of my tunic. "Nothing. Maybe I am worrying."

"Over what?"

I look at my mate. God, he's gorgeous. I love everything about him, from the hard lines of his mouth to the arch of his horns. I love the intense glow of his eyes when he gazes at me. I love the sight of his big hand on my belly, and my heart squeezes with fear all over again. What if he decides that I'm not enough for him—like my parents did—and abandons me? "Are you happy?" I ask, my heart aching.

This time, he gives me a slow, brilliant smile. "Why would I not be happy? I have a beautiful mate, two healthy kits, and one on the way." He pauses and gives me a sly look. "Or three."

I smile.

He reaches up and rubs a knuckle along the line of my jaw. "Josee, you are my heart. I love nothing more than your laughter and it hurts me to see you worry. Tell me what is wrong so I can fix it."

I love this man so much. I know it's my old insecurities rising up. I know Haeden adores me and the babies. I know he would never abandon us like my parents abandoned me. This isn't Earth and he's not a human man. He thinks differently. I know all this. I do. It's just my brain and my old emotional baggage working against me.

"You'd tell me if you were unhappy, wouldn't you?" I ask him. "Because I'm so happy that sometimes it scares me."

"If I were unhappy, you would know. Am I good at hiding my emotions?" He tilts his head, giving me his most "Haeden" look, and I have to smother a giggle. He's got a point—he's about as good at hiding his displeasure as I am at hiding, well, anything. We're both transparent as glass.

"Good point."

He leans forward and presses a gentle kiss to my lips. "You are my mate. You and my kits are everything to me."

I hold him close as his mouth brushes over mine in the most delicate of kisses. He's so careful with me, I realize. He's strong as could be, and I'm half his size, but I've never felt unsafe or like he would accidentally hurt me. He's always so cautious, so courteous. I love that about him, but tonight I wish he'd just grab me and drag my clothes off so he can fuck me silly. "Haeden," I whisper against his lips, about to make that very suggestion.

Haeden's hand steals up to one breast, teasing the nipple under my tunic. His gaze is so hot with its intensity that I feel achy and liquid all over. "Mmm?"

God, I love the rumble of his voice.

"Mommy?"

I freeze.

"What is it, Joden?" Haeden asks, his hand sliding back out of my tunic just as quickly.

"I wet the bed," Joden says, sniffling. He rubs a fist in one eye. "And now I can't sleep 'cause there's peepee everywhere."

"Aww, baby. Don't cry." My heart wrings for my little man, and all sexy thoughts are forgotten as being a parent takes over. I reach out to touch Joden's little hand and Haeden's already climbing out of the bed. "Papa's going to fix it for you, okay? Let's get you some fresh jammies while Papa makes a new bed for you." It just means more laundry to do in the morning, and doing laundry in the brutal season is awful, but Joden's my baby, and I can't be mad.

As Haeden strips the bedding, I sit up in the furs and help Joden change out of his wet pajamas. We do a quick sponge bath and then he's in fresh jammies, and before Haeden is even finished making his bed, Joden crawls in next to me and curls up against me.

"Can I sleep wif you, Mommy?"

"You can for a little bit," I tell him, holding him against my big stomach and knowing that he's probably going to end up staying in bed with us all night. It's something we're trying to break him of, but it hasn't been easy.

He curls up against me and his hair smells like soap and my baby boy and his little horns tuck under my chin perfectly. I hold him close and watch as Haeden pulls rolled up furs out of storage and makes a new bed for our son, but my eyes close and I'm falling asleep before he's done.

The furs shift, and I realize I've nodded off. Haeden moves behind me, pressing up against my back and spooning me from behind. His arm goes around my belly and he kisses my shoulder. "Go back to sleep, my heart."

Joden's still curled up against my front, fast asleep. "Should we let him stay or put him back to bed?"

Haeden sighs and glances down at our son. He brushes a lock of hair off of Joden's brow and I can see the love for him in his eyes. "He can stay, but only for tonight."

I smile wryly at my mate, because we've had this same conversation a dozen times and each time we wake up with Joden in our bed.

Children change everything, they really do. But as Haeden presses one more kiss to my shoulder and settles down against me, I can feel the heat of his cock burning against my buttock. If Joden hadn't interrupted, we would have had sex. Great sex, even if it was me-heavily-pregnant sex. But Joden's here in our bed, and it's only a matter of time before Joha wakes up and wants to nurse, and then the new baby will be here by the time she's weaned and....

There's got to be a balance in there somewhere, isn't there? Room for me and Haeden to be a mated couple as well as parents? Now, more than ever before, I'm determined to make this silly lingerie and show my mate I can still be sexy.

4

HASSEN

A few days later

By the end of this day, I will see my mate and my kit again. I cannot stop grinning as I watch Ver-on-cah adjust the saddle strapped to Ashtar's gigantic beast shoulders. The golden male is in his "drakoni" form and is readying to fly me and Cashol back to Croatoan village, where my Mah-dee will be waiting for me, Masan in her arms.

I cannot wait to see her eyes light up, to see my son reach out for me with excited small hands. I cannot wait for my mate's small hands, either, and I grin to myself once more. I am excited to see my son, of course, but my body is crying out for private time with my mate. My cock is more than ready to return to her. There are good people at this camp, but ah, I am ready to return home. Just thinking about it makes me yawn again.

"Why do you keep yawning, brother?" Cashol asks. Ver-on-cah glances back at us.

"I am sleepy."

He snorts, as if this amuses him. "You slept all day yesterday. And you elected not to go hunting with Thrand because you had to nap the day before. Why all the sleeping?"

"I am saving my strength," I tell him proudly. "Once I am home, my Mah-dee will wear me out."

"Ew," Ver-on-cah calls out. "I did not want to hear that." The big dragon rumbles, as if sharing her amusement.

Cashol just grunts. "I am ready to see my Meh-gan. It has been far too long since I have held her or hugged my son." He has been here as long as I have, and we are the last to head back. All of the others have already returned or have had their mates brought to them. We are the last two, and while I have not minded helping, I am more than ready to return to my mate and kit.

It has been hard to be without Mah-dee for so long. She fills my dreams at night, and I wake up missing the rounded curves of her body and her sultry smile. She is incredible, my mate, and has always known exactly what she wanted. I love that about her, and how she's just as fierce out of the furs as she is in them. I tell Cashol this, too, but he just rolls his eyes. Everyone has heard my Mah-dee stories over and over again. It has become a bit of a joke around the Icehome camp. The others do not want to ask me questions because they know I will bring up my mate in the conversation. Part of some "alien bingo card" as Bree-shit likes to joke. I do not know what this means, though.

Mah-dee would know.

I do not care if they find my constant mentions of her irritating. I adore my mate and think she is perfect. I love her fire and her wily mind. I love the soft yellow curls of her mane...and the ones on her cunt. I love her big round thighs and the soft pillows of her teats. I love all of her, and talking about her makes it seem like she is less far away...so I talk about her often.

But soon she will be in my arms again. And I grin like a fool at Cashol.

"Saddle's on," Vuh-ron-cah says, and puts a gloved hand on Ashtar's beast shoulder. "Any last goodbyes or are we ready to get going?" She tugs a hat over her head and pulls a thick scarf over her mouth to protect it. The flight is hard on humans, especially when we go over the mountains and it grows increasingly cold, but Vuh-ron-cah will not let Ashtar go without her, so I am grateful she has volunteered.

"I have said all my goodbyes," I tell her cheerfully. "Show me where to put my pack and I am ready to go."

"I as well," Cashol adds. "I am ready to return to my mate and son. They have been without me long enough."

"Let's get this show on the road, then," Vuh-ron-cah says. "I'll show you guys how to set up the baskets you're going to be riding in, and then you're going to want to bundle up. It's gonna be a long ride."

"That sounds like something my Mah-dee would say," I tease them.

"Gross," Vuh-ron-cah says, and Cashol curls his lip at my joke.

"What?" It is not funny?

I thought it was funny.

Mah-dee would think it was funny.

I sigh. I am ready to return to her. I hunger for her smile and the wicked sparkle in her eyes. Of all people, Mah-dee understands me more than anyone.

♥

THE DAY IS long and just as cold as the human female predicted. When we cross over the mountains, the air gets so cold it steals my breath, and I shield my face with layers of furs. It means I cannot see the ground far below, which is just as well. Looking down at such a tall height makes me queasy, and when I glance over at Cashol's basket, he is hunched low. The ride is a miserable one, and only Vuh-ron-cah seems to be enjoying herself. I occasionally catch her laughter on the wind, as if she is amused by a private conversation no one can hear.

But then the suns set behind the horizon, and the chilly air gets even colder. My lashes are icicles and the scarf over my mouth crusts with more ice. My exposed skin burns against the cold wind...but then Vuh-ron-cah points ahead, and I can barely make out the shadowed crescent of the gorge that holds our people's home. The village is close.

And the realization that my mate will be in my arms soon makes me warm.

It feels as if it takes forever for Ashtar to gently set down on the ground above the crevasse. He finally lands and hunches low. Vuh-ron-cah slides off her saddle and the dragon immediately extends his wings again, using them to protect her from the blasting wind. Cashol and I manage to climb out of our baskets, and my feet feel as if they are made entirely of ice. I stomp them on the snow to bring feeling back to my toes, and by the time we pull the saddles and trappings off of Ashtar's back, Zennek, Bek and Haeden have come up the lift to greet us. We greet each other with quick slaps on the back and a clasping of arms, and they take our packs from us as Vuh-ron-cah holds a fur cloak out to the big dragon. A moment later, Ashtar is in his human form and hunched on the ground, naked. He takes the cloak from his mate and tosses it around her instead, kissing her brow. She sputters.

"I am full of fire," he explains simply, grinning. "I do not need a blanket. My mate, on the other hand, is cold."

"Pants," she says sharply. "You need pants."

"All these moons and you still cannot make him wear clothing?" Bek says, sounding more lighthearted than I remember. He claps Ashtar on the shoulder. "Your mate is right, though. Some of the human females are skittish about seeing another's mate nude." He takes his lightweight cloak off and offers it to Ashtar, who wraps it around his hips.

Bek is...so happy. I stare at him, astonished. Sometimes I forget that he has a mate now, and because of her he is content. I am glad for him. Everyone should be as happy as I am with my Mah-dee. Who should be...right below. I grab my pack and head for the lift, eager to have my arms around her once more. I cannot wait to see her face...and to see my son. Cashol and I have the same idea, and he gives me a playful mock-shove as we both get onto the lift at the same time and then release the pulley to go down.

All other reunions can wait except one.

The path to the village that winds through the gorge seems never-ending, but eventually I can hear happy cries and see a crowd gathering up ahead. Cashol breaks into a run, and his mate races forward, sobbing happily. She has her arms out, and Cashol grabs her about the waist and swings her around, laughing. I did not realize until now just how much he missed her, but when I pass him there are tears of joy in his eyes as he presses a thousand kisses on his mate's face. A young male races out and for a moment, I think it is Masan, but this one has large horns and deep blue skin—Holvek, who is the spitting image of his father. He flings himself on his hugging mother and father, and they add him into their tearful embrace.

I scan the crowd for my mate and son. Mah-dee did not rush out and scream with tears at the sight of me, but I did not expect that. My Mah-dee is not like Meh-gan, who clings to Cashol as if he is life itself. My mate is independent and confident and would expect me to come to her. I grin, imagining a look of amusement on my beautiful mate's face as she watches Meh-gan blubber and weep all over Cashol.

A heavily cloaked figure steps forward, and she has her hands on a little boy in front of her. The female is heavier than the others that stand near her, teats large and tenting the front of her tunic. My heart begins to pound. For a moment, I feel like Cashol's female in that I want to weep at the sight. Because I know who that is, even before she drops her hood and reveals her yellow mane and round, smiling face.

It is my beautiful, perfect Mah-dee.

A huge knot forms in my throat and I swallow hard even as I stagger forward. Masan races forward, his arms out, and I snatch him up as he crashes toward me. The emotion clogging my throat turns to laughter, and I hug my son close. He has grown since I last saw him, I think. He looks bigger, and his shaggy mane is longer. "My little hunter," I murmur. "Have you been taking care of your mama for me?"

"Of course, Papa!" He beams up at me. "And I have a pet dirtbeak!"

I try to hide my reaction to that. "Do you, now?"

But then Mah-dee arrives, a teasing smile on her pink lips, and my heart surges again. I tug Masan onto my side, freeing an arm, and put it around my mate, hugging her close. My embrace is full of my family, and this feels…indescribable. As if I could scale the mountains themselves.

"Welcome home," Mah-dee says into my ear, her voice throaty.

My cock immediately grows hard. I squeeze her closer, liking that her large teats push against my side and her hand goes to my chest. "I have missed you greatly, my beautiful mate."

She laughs. "Of course you did. We're awesome." She winks at Masan and wraps her arms around my waist, holding me tightly. "You can never stay away that long again, all right?"

"Did you miss me?"

She tosses her lovely yellow mane. "I would never admit such a thing." But there's a smile on her lips and her eyes sparkle so brightly that for a moment, they look shiny. I wonder if she is going to weep like Meh-gan, but she just bites her lip and pulls me in for another tight hug.

I hold her close, my eyes shut as I simply drink in the pleasure of being reunited with my family. My Mah-dee is in my arms, with hers wrapped around me. My son is healthy and strong. Truly, I am the luckiest of hunters. "I did not miss you either," I tease.

"Lies," Mah-dee says, grinning. She sniffs, getting her composure. "Stacy's cooking up a feast and there's going to be a big celebration tonight for you and the others."

"And hraku seeds!" my son says happily. He has a "sweet tooth" as Mah-dee calls it.

My mate laughs, and the sound is beautiful. "Yes, with hraku seeds!" She beams up at me and then grabs my braid and yanks it slightly, tugging my ear down. "And you and I are going to have a private celebration tonight as soon as we can slip away."

"We are?"

"Oh yes." Her eyes gleam with promise. "I'm going to show you how much I missed you."

My cock jerks in my breeches, and my sac grows tight. "Keep talking like that and I will have to change my leggings," I warn her, glad for the layers that hide my discomfort from the rest of the tribe that's approaching to greet us.

She just winks at me, sultry and playful, and I cannot wait to be alone with her once more.

5

HASSEN

Just as my Mah-dee promised, there is a celebration. Pashov's mate Stay-see, Asha, and Kemli take charge of the food, doling out large portions of a slow-roasted dvisti stuffed with fresh herbs and seeds. The meat is tender and falls off the bone, and I groan with pleasure at every bite. Most of the cooking back at the Icehome camp is from a practical standpoint or necessity, and they do not take the time to pit-roast a dvisti for two days with herbs like Stay-see does. There are drums, and stories, and new kits to admire—Rokan's new daughter looks just like him. Shorshie's belly grows larger, as does Jo-see's, and Vuh-ron-ca sits with Maylak, their heads close together as they share a private discussion. Pregnant Mehgan sits in Cashol's lap and clings to him as if he will disappear again. My Mah-dee does not—probably because Masan has taken over my lap—but she remains close and touches me often, her eyes promising wonderful things. I watch with contentment as Suh-mer and Kate bring out pots of paint and declare they will paint faces, and all the kits line up with excitement to get their turn.

As Mah-dee gets me another helping of food, I talk to my chief. I tell him how things are at the Icehome camp, how An-shee has given birth to a red-hued daughter and taken Vordis as her mate. How the islanders get better at hunting all the time. Shren and Will-uh's return. How Leezh and Har-loh have both given birth to girls as well. How Raahosh and R'jaal have both taken on the mantle of leadership over the squabbling groups.

Vektal is pleased to hear that. "Perhaps I will not have to go back soon." His gaze lingers on his mate, who seems thinner than before, and I know he wants to stay at her side.

"If they need more help, I will go back," I promise. "But I will take my mate and son with me this time." I do not plan on leaving them for such a long time ever again.

"Hopefully that will not be necessary," Vektal says. "If they cannot be an independent tribe as they wish, it might be wiser for them to come here." He rubs his chin, thinking. "We will see what the bitter season brings."

Mah-dee clears her throat and leans over my shoulder, her mane swaying. "Are you two done talking?"

I glance over at my chief and he just grins, knowing. He gets up and approaches his mate, putting his arms around her as she talks to Jo-see. I turn to Mah-dee. "Now we are done."

She wiggles her brows at me, her hand going to the front of my tunic. She grabs a handful of it and tugs at me, indicating I should get to my feet. "Masan is getting his other cheek painted, and then Summer's going to keep him and Rollan busy for a while. They're spending the night over at her place tonight. That means you and I get to privately celebrate."

Ah, my cunning mate. I grin, getting to my feet. "A private celebration of what kind?"

"Valentine's Day," she tells me.

I...was hoping she would say mating of some kind. Tongue mating, cunt and cock mating...my tongue on her cunt mating, her tongue on my cock mating...any kind of mating, really. "What is Val-en-time?"

"Valentine," she corrects, and takes my hand. "And I'll tell you about it as we go to our hut, okay? Or do you want to stay at the party?" She tosses her yellow mane and gives me a playful look.

Stay and eat instead of pleasuring my mate? I snort at the idea. "You know there is nowhere I would rather be than between your legs, my pretty one."

"I'm trying to eat here," Nora says, shooting me a horrified look. She is seated a few paces away with Dagesh, who just grins like a fool. He understands.

Mah-dee giggles with pleasure and pulls me away. "Follow me and let me tell you all about the human tradition of Valentine's Day, my big, sexy barbarian."

"I like this already," I murmur as she leads me away from the group. I should have known that my Mah-dee would have something exciting planned. She is an unpredictable, bold female, and it is just one of the many reasons why she has my heart.

"Papa?" Masan's little voice carries above the laughter of the tribe. "Where are you going?"

My mate freezes, wincing. "I'll let you handle this, Papa," she says and gestures at me.

I release her hand and crouch low, pulling my son into my arms. I hug him close, inhaling his scent. I cherish my son, and I love how big he's getting. He is clever, my boy. "Papa is going to spend alone time with Mama right now. Give me a hug and I promise we will go hunting together in the morning, yes?"

Mah-dee clears her throat. "Afternoon."

"Afternoon," I correct, and I like this even more. Her plans will keep us busy for a while, and excitement builds in my belly. I focus on my son's solemn face. "But tonight you will spend time with your friends, yes?"

A smile curves his rounded cheeks. "Okay, Papa." He flings his arms around my neck and presses kisses to my face. "I'm glad you're home."

"I am, too," I say, and there is a curious knot in my throat.

"Don't forget to come get me tomorrow," he says as he pulls away.

"I would never forget," I vow to him, and I mean it. Spending time with my son is just as special as spending time with my mate. "Now, go give Mama a kiss and go back to the party."

He beams at me and then flings his arms around Mah-dee and kisses her before racing back to join the others. She has a smear of green paint on her nose when she looks at me, and I chuckle, wiping it away. "Now your face is painted like a kit's."

"Maybe we should paint *your* face."

"Bah." When she does not laugh, I grow a little worried. "You are not taking me away to paint my face...are you?" Maybe I will like this Val-time less than I thought.

"Not your face, no," she says, a wicked smile on her face.

That does not reassure me. "What, then?"

She simply takes my hand. "Let me tell you all about Valentine's Day. It's February 14th back on Earth, and it's a day that you show your love to your significant other. You give each other gifts and make sure you spend quality time together."

"So it is like the other haul-day when you show you care for someone by refusing to poison them?" I grow suspicious as she leads me back to our hut, because this sounds a bit like the other haul-days that humans celebrate. All of them sound alike—gifts are given, mates are appreciated, and people feast.

"No," she says patiently. "This one is very specifically about love. Romantic love between a man and a woman." Our boots crunch in the snow and she shivers under her many layers. "Man, it is cold tonight."

I automatically take off my over-wrap and tuck it around her. "You are surprised by the cold every brutal season," I tease her. Right now she is wearing so many layers she looks like an overfed metlak. It is adorable.

"So I do." She gives me a sly look as we approach our hut. "Are you ready for your present?"

"More than ready." Mah-dee is impossible to predict and I am excited to see what she has made for me.

With a sultry smile, she leads me inside.

I look around our hut eagerly, but I do not see anything new right away. Perhaps she has hidden it, then. I wait for her to show me, but she only pulls me towards our furs and then gestures that I should sit down. "Let me help you take off your boots."

We peel my layers off and then I wear nothing but my breech-cloth. My cock is hard, straining against the leather with the nearness of my mate, but she does not seem to be in a hurry to join me. Instead, she moves to the area of the hut she calls her "kitchen" and pulls out a small bottle. "I've been hiding this," she tells me, her voice full of promise. "Want to know what it is?"

"I do." I lean back on the furs, propping up on one arm so I can see better. "Show me."

She hands the bottle to me instead.

Curious, I pull the stopper out and sniff it. It smells...sweet. "Hraku?"

"Hraku syrup," she corrects, and looks proud. "I made it just for tonight."

"...Oh." I will never understand the human fascination with sweet things. I cannot stand the taste. To me, if things are sweet, it reminds me of the cloying smell of rotting meat. "My thanks?"

She giggles and taps a fingertip on my nose. "It's for me, silly."

"Oh?" I am curious as to why she handed it to me, but at least I do not have to eat it. "Part of the Val-time tradition?"

"It can be part of ours," Mah-dee says in a throaty voice, and then tosses off one layer of clothing, then another. She casts off her furs and I watch with great interest, ready for her to be naked so we can mate.

But when she gets down to her last layer, I am...confused. I stare in surprise at the form-fitting leathers. Tiny straps cross over opposite shoulders, framing her deep cleavage. Her teats are covered in white fur that barely seems adequate for support, and her waist is nipped in tightly. I can see a band of her pale skin just above the tiny furry white loincloth she wears over her cunt. This is...new.

"Do you like?" Mah-dee puts her hands on her hips and shifts, leaning forward and then her prominent teats look even more prominent.

I study her clothing, shocked at the sight of it. Why does it cling so tightly to her? Why does it make my cock so hard to see this? "It does not look very practical," I admit.

She giggles. "That's the point, silly." She cups her breasts and then gives them an eye-widening jiggle. "Do you like it?"

"I do not think so," I say slowly. "I would not like for others to see you dressed like this. Your teats are too...big and bouncy." My hands itch to touch them. "And your loincloth barely covers the curls of your cunt." I look up at her, frowning. "I do not know if you should wear this, my mate."

She gives another snort-giggle, her mouth curving with amusement. "It's not meant to be worn out in public, silly. It's meant to be worn just for you, in the privacy of our furs."

"Oh." I stare at it again, at the fascinating expanse of her cleavage and the contrast to her tightly bound waist. "*Oh.* In that case, I like this very much."

Mah-dee glances down at my crotch. "I can see that." She looks up, winks at me, and then tugs on one of the ties at my hip. "I see that you like this more than the syrup."

"I am confused about the syrup," I admit, unable to take my eyes off of her spectacularly large teats. That white fur and those tiny straps...clothing should not be so fascinating, should it? But I am entranced at the sight of the creamy swells of her teats that rise and fall with every breath she takes.

"Like I said," she murmurs, and pulls my loincloth off. "It's for me." A deep sigh escapes her at the sight of my cock. "God, I've missed you."

"It has missed you, as well." I reach out to caress one large teat, unable to resist the nearness of that fur-covered mound. "All of me has."

She takes the syrup from me and then puts a hand on my chest, pushing me back onto the furs. I go eagerly, because I know nothing but good things come when I am on my back and my aroused mate is looming over me. As I watch, she presses a kiss to my raised knee, and because she is not paying attention, some of the syrup dribbles out onto my cock.

"You spilled it," I point out. "Should I get a towel?"

Mah-dee sits up, and there is a smile on her face. "You really don't know how this game is played, do you? God, you're so cute."

Then, she takes my syrup-covered cock and sucks the tip clean.

I fall back against the furs, groaning. *Now* I understand this game. "Are you…going to lick everywhere there is syrup?" I ask, panting hard.

"Mmmhmm."

I take the bottle from her hand and douse my cock with it, shaking the thick droplets free until they cover my sac and lower. I love it when Mah-dee's tongue goes exploring.

She giggles with delight, and then gets to work on cleaning me with her mouth. I groan, dropping the near-empty bottle as her slick little human tongue works over my cock, then my sac, and further still. She flicks it over every crevice and fold, teasing and sucking and making little noises of pleasure as she cleans me with her mouth. Her hands are sticky and her lips are, too, but her breathless little moans—and her busy tongue that goes places tongues are not meant to go—are too much for me to take and I thrust up against her when she takes my cock into her mouth. I need to come, and come hard. "Mah-dee," I warn, but she takes me deep, giving me silent acknowledgement that she is ready.

With a snarl, I pump into her mouth, filling it with my seed. She makes a sound of encouragement, and then pulls back, my release spilling down her chin as she struggles to keep up.

"My mate," I tell her, touching her face as she nuzzles and licks me clean. "Oh, how I have missed you."

Mah-dee just chuckles and then sits up, stretching. "Let me get you a towel and I'll finish cleaning you off."

"Is there anything left?" I pant, amused.

"Well, I plan on climbing you to get mine, and I'm not about to give myself a raging yeast infection." She gets to her feet, tosses me a satisfied little look over her shoulder, and saunters over to the kitchen, that strange, furry loincloth barely containing the globes of her glorious bottom. She rejoins me a few moments later, taking a ladle of heated water from over the banked fire and adding it to the cold water in her bowl. With a swish, she adds a bit of soapberry and then begins to wash me as if I am helpless.

I have to admit, it makes my cock stir. "Do I get to wash you next?" I ask, lying back and enjoying the view of her glorious teats as she runs the warm towel over my loins.

"I'm not dirty…yet." And she gives me a promising look.

"Yet," I agree. I eye her strange clothing with approval. If I am the only one that gets to see her like this, I like it far more than I originally thought. "Will you wear these furs for me whenever I ask?"

"As often as you like."

"No wonder you were cold. I thought we would sneak out and mate behind someone's hut in secret like we normally do." I grin at the memories.

"It's no fun if they're not there to hear, and everyone's at the longhouse."

I chuckle. "Maybe I shall take you to the longhouse later, then."

"Maybe so." She washes me higher, her hands resting on my chest for a moment before she moves on.

That seems odd to me. "I did not get dirty on my chest, my mate."

She shrugs. "I was just…seeing if your cootie was waking up. Seeing if we'd resonate again when we reunited. Aehako and Kira did the moment they got back together." She puts the washtowel in the bowl and sets it aside, the look on her face hard to read. "It's baby number two for them."

"So I heard. I am glad for them." When she does not respond, I reach out and take her hand in mine, then tug her rounded form down in the furs so her grand teats rest against my chest. "Does this make you sad?"

"I…don't know. Pretty soon we might be the only ones in the village that only have one kit." I open my mouth to speak and she immediately puts a finger over my lips. "Before you say it, I know Bek and Elly and Kate and the others are just newly pregnant. I mean of…us. The old crew. The ones that have been here a while. Almost everyone has a second baby on the way. Heck, Josie's got a third. And…I don't know how that makes me feel. I don't want you to think I'm less of a mate because I'm not crapping out babies at every turn."

I snort, because she must be joking…but her face is solemn. "Mah-dee. How can you think such things?"

"Well, it's easy," she retorts and taps a finger on the side of my brow. "I use this big hunk of meat up here. You should try it sometime."

I just grin, because I like her ferocity. "You could never be less of a mate. In fact, you are probably more mate than any hunter can handle…except me." I can tell this pleases her because her mouth quirks in a little smile. I continue, because I want that smile to grow. "If you and I never resonate again, it does not matter to me. If we only have Masan, then I will be thrilled because he is now old enough to spend the night with Suh-mer and Warrek, and that means I have more play time with my mate." I move one tiny strap of her leathers to the side and a large, juicy teat slides free, her nipple revealed to me. I take it between thumb and forefinger, rolling it back and forth to tease her. I love the way her eyes darken with need and how she presses her teat into my hand, demanding more. "And if we resonate again, I will be happy to have more kits so Masan can have a sister or a brother to take over to Suh-mer and Warrek when he goes."

She giggles, her expression soft as she gazes down at me. "God, I love you."

"I love as well," I tell her, using her human words that she likes to hear. "We will resonate again in time. Or not. It does not matter to me as long as I have you in my arms. Our son is strong and healthy. Your teats are glorious and begging for my touch. Let us not rush things and simply enjoy each day as it comes."

"That sounds good to me," she says, breathless as I pinch her nipple. She pants with need, and then a sly look enters her eyes. "And...I bet Bek and Elly didn't stay at the celebration long. I bet even now they're back in their hut."

"Mmm...we have not mated behind their hut, have we?" I know my Mah-dee likes the thrill of it, the danger of being caught by another as I bury myself inside her. She loves to brace her hands on the hard stones of their wall as I drive into her, biting back her cries of pleasure.

I admit, I like the sight of that, too. Sometimes she is not quiet enough and we get caught...which I also like, because she comes immediately when it happens, her cunt gripping my cock like a vise. Those are the best times.

The thought makes my cock stir back to life, and I eye her strange clothing. "Will you be warm enough with a cloak over that?"

"One way to find out," she says, eyes gleaming.

We gaze at each other for a moment, and then scramble for our cloaks.

6

JOSIE

We're leaving the longhouse, Joha asleep in Haeden's arms, as a low cry carries across the quiet village.

"Yes! Like that!"

Haeden makes a harrumph in his throat and turns to look at me. "I see Mah-dee and Hassen are up to their old tricks."

I can't help but smile at my mate's sour expression. "They're just having a good time. It's fine."

"You say that because they are behind Bek's hut this time and not ours." He touches Joha's round baby cheek with a tender finger and my heart squeezes in my chest. "If they get any louder, they will wake this little one up."

He's such a wonderful father. I love seeing Joha cuddled against his chest, her thumb in her mouth as he carefully pulls one of the fur blankets higher to shield her from the chilly air. We don't get much wind down here in the canyon, but it doesn't mean that it's not breath-stealingly cold.

I pretend to stomp my boot against the cobblestones to adjust it, but in reality, I'm listening to Maddie and Hassen get it on in the distance. He must have liked her lingerie, I think wistfully. I helped her put on the final stitches early this morning. She made a simple corset and a teeny tiny bra with crisscross straps and equally tiny panties of soft white fur. Nothing crazy, but she assured me that Hassen would love it, and I could tell she was practically beside herself with glee.

My "lingerie" is simpler. It's more of a babydoll made out of the thinnest leather I could find, trimmed with fur and cinched at the breasts so it'll lift and separate the girls. I'm still breastfeeding, so they're big already, but my figure doesn't compare to Maddie's. I wonder if it'll even be worth it, considering how pregnant I am and that I'm not even close to giving birth.

Man, when did I turn into such a downer? No wonder Haeden doesn't want to sleep with me. I give the back of my hand a slap to mentally chide myself for being so negative, and when I look up, my mate has paused to wait for me, and he's studying me with a quizzical look on his face. "Jo-see?" His voice is low and husky so as not to wake our daughter. "Is all well?"

I smile brightly at him, stepping forward and putting my hand at the crook of his arm like I normally do. "Why wouldn't everything be well?"

"You seem distracted tonight." He studies my face. "Do you feel well? Is your stomach upset?"

"I'm fine, really."

Haeden knows me better than anyone else, so I'm not entirely surprised when he gives me another skeptical glance. Maybe I have been a little quiet and distracted tonight. I've been thinking about my mate and how to approach seducing him without looking ridiculously pregnant. I'm not as brave and bold as Maddie with her entire Valentine-slash-seduction plan. I'd feel silly tying Haeden's hands and having my way with him like Maddie suggested. The sex between us has always been good—okay, amazing—and we've never needed to resort to crazy stuff to spice things up.

Maybe that's part of the problem, I'm realizing. Maybe he's bored with me because I'm not as bold as I used to be?

"You are frowning," my mate chides. "Come, Jo-see, confess what bothers you."

"I promise it's nothing."

He grunts. "I do not like these secrets," he whispers, pitching his voice low so we don't wake Joha. "We will talk more when she is in her furs." My mate pauses and narrows his eyes at me. "Is there a reason why you sent Joden with Suh-mer and Warrek?"

"I told you. Masan and Rollan are having a sleepover with them and I thought it would be fun for Joden to join in. Summer said she didn't mind." I wanted to send Joha, too, but my little one is still nursing and that means she can get fussy if she's hungry. She's an independent sleeper, though, which means there's no chance of her crawling into bed with us...which is the main reason why Joden's with Summer tonight.

Haeden gives me another curious look but says nothing. We get to our hut, and I can no longer hear Hassen and Maddie in their furtive rendezvous. I hope she's having fun and loving the lingerie she worked so hard on. Haeden pulls the screen back and helps me duck inside, and once I've taken two steps in, he puts a hand to the small of my back and steers me toward the best seat by the fire. "Sit, my heart."

"The fire is almost out," I protest. "And Joha—"

He presses a quick kiss to the top of my head. "I will take care of all of it. You are tired. Sit."

I do sit down and fight back a sigh as I watch him move around the hut, preparing things with one hand, his other arm full of our daughter. He puts on a pouch of tea and grabs the fuel tongs, tossing another dung chip onto the fire and stirring the coals. With that done, he moves to the front of the hut, secures the screen, and then moves to settle Joha in her bed. It's an oversized square basket full of the softest furs, and my girl's a hard sleeper. She barely stirs as her father sets her down...and then checks her leathers. I know without looking that they'll be wet—habit—and I'm not surprised when Haeden immediately pulls out the small trunk that I keep her diaper-wraps in and begins to change her. Joha sleeps on, her thumb in her mouth, her dark hair curling around her sweet baby face.

I watch my mate, entranced, my heart aching with love for him. He's such a good dad. He takes care of my little girl without being asked, because he knows it's a struggle for me to juggle both kits and still do the household chores. It doesn't matter if he spends all day hunting, he always makes sure to help me out when he's home. And it's easy to see that he loves the children so, so much.

So what is it that's off between us and how can I fix it?

I think of Maddie and her "Valentine" private party. She never doubts that her mate will find her incredibly sexy. Granted, she's also not on baby number three, but I need to take a page from her book. Haeden loves me and we have a wonderful family. I just need to reignite our fading spark. With that in mind, I get up and move toward the screened off area that functions as our "private" bedroom. "I think I'm going to get ready for bed," I say, faking a yawn.

He nods, his hands full of Joha and her dirty wraps.

I watch him for a moment longer, my heart full of love for him and my sweet little girl, and then I decide to do this thing. I go behind the screen, pull out my new nightie and change quickly. I run a hand through my freshly washed hair and then comb the waves out so they fall over my shoulders in what I hope is a sexy manner. Maddie suggested perfume or even a pot of berry-stained lip balm, but Haeden would look at me as if I was crazy if I wore that stuff. I love my man, but he's definitely not a fan of fuss. So instead, I arrange myself atop the blankets and try to look sexy and eager. I adjust the bow digging in under my breasts, trying to make my cleavage look more bountiful as Haeden moves around in the hut on the other side of the screen. I hear him wash his hands in a bowl of water, and then his footsteps as he approaches. I toss my hair quickly, bite my lips so they look pink, and ready my most seductive expression.

Haeden appears, drying his hands on a fur towel, and eyes my leather babydoll outfit. The tiny straps are already straining and probably won't last multiple wearings, and the fur on the hem tickles my knees. "Your tunic is strange."

That's it? That's all I get? "Do you like it?" I lean forward, trying to get him to eye my cleavage without pressing my weight on my belly.

"It does not seem very warm. Are you hot? Should I bank the fire?" He tosses the towel down on the floor (which I ignore) and begins to remove his boots.

"It's not meant to be warm," I tell him, playing with the tie between my breasts. "It's meant to be sexy."

"Sexy?" Haeden stares at me for a long moment. "Why? What brings this about?"

All of his questions are making me doubt myself, and I sit up, feeling self-conscious and weird. "I was trying to seduce you, but I guess I'm not very good at it. Never mind." I just feel tired and sad, suddenly. Like I've done something wrong and I don't know what it is.

"Jo-see, my heart," Haeden murmurs, and sits down on the furs next to me. He cups my chin in one big hand and tilts my face up so my eyes meet his. "There is something you are not telling me. Why do you wish to seduce me when you are obviously tired and not feeling well?"

"Maybe I'm not that tired," I say defensively. "Maybe I'm worried about us."

"Us?" He looks genuinely surprised. "What is wrong with us?" He caresses my cheek, his gaze so tender it's making me feel all kinds of things.

I almost feel silly saying it aloud. "Joden says we don't tickle anymore. He told me that you said I'm always pregnant and we don't tickle and you only want more babies because I do." My lower lip quivers as I remember the hurt of those words. "And you know he repeats everything he hears."

Haeden just shakes his head, his free hand going to my waist and his arm loops around me, supporting me as he pulls me against him. "My beautiful mate. You worry far too much."

"But what he says is true. We don't tickle—I mean, have sex—anymore. We haven't had sex in a full turn of the moon!"

"And do you remember what happened in the last moon?" he asks, leaning down and pressing a gentle kiss to the tip of my nose. "Your stomach was upset for the last few days. You vomited many times. And just before that, Joha ate that plant and her stomach was very angry. And before that...you had a sour stomach once more. This kit has been harder on you, my sweet mate. I can see the exhaustion on your face when I look at you. Why would I come after you and attack you with my needs when you are already struggling?"

"Because I'm so irresistible you can't help yourself?" I ask brightly, knowing that everything he says is true. I have been sick a lot, and then Joha made herself ill, and it's just been a mess lately. "Sometimes I wish you *would* attack me with your needs. Harassment is sexy as long as it comes from you. I mean, sometimes a girl needs her ass grabbed, you know?"

"You do? Why?"

"Because you can't resist my ass? Because I'm so sexy it blows your mind and you can't go another moment without touching me?" I know I'm asking a lot. My Haeden is a wonderful dad and mate, but he's a bit...taciturn. He's not prone to constant kissing and squeezing like Maddie and Hassen, who, even after years of being mated, can't keep their hands off each other. Haeden's more private. Which is not a bad thing. "I guess I'm just being needy."

"Jo-see," Haeden murmurs again. There's exasperation in his eyes, but also love. He leans in and kisses my mouth, ever so lightly, and I want to just melt against him. "I am not your human family. I will never abandon you. You must put those fears away once and for all."

"It's just...hard." I know I have baggage that pops up every now and then. All I've ever wanted is to have someone that loves me, and now that I have it, I worry I'm going to lose it.

"If you wish for me to grab your ass in front of others, I will."

"It's not that I want that. I just want...I don't know. For you to be overpowered with lust for me! Like we were before!"

His mouth quirks, his warm breath playing over my face as he gently strokes a thumb along my jaw. "You think I am no longer overpowered with lust for you?"

"We haven't had sex in a month," I feel the need to tactfully point out again.

"That does not mean my feelings have changed. Shall I grab at you every time I have a lustful thought about my beautiful, fragile mate? You will not be able to walk because my hands will be on you, constantly."

I like the sound of that. Heck, just picturing that makes me wet. I cling to him. "Go on."

"We are not all over each other constantly because there are two kits to be taken care of and one on the way. That does change things, but not in a bad way." He slides his knuckles gently down to my collarbone and then over to the strap of my nightie, easing it down my shoulder. "It just means I must learn to be patient even if my cock aches with need, because it is important to me that you are happy and whole."

"I'm happy when we touch, too," I whisper, entranced at his tenderness. This is what I've been aching for. I've been craving intimacy with my Haeden, and I'm so glad I spoke up.

He chuckles. "I am, as well, but I also watch out for my sweet mate, who would run herself ragged trying to be the best mother to my son, who is exhausting enough for three mothers, and my daughter, who is easier but still needs much attention."

"Do I?"

"You do," he says firmly. "But if it means so much to you, I will tell you all the times in a day I think about mating you. How often I think about getting to our furs and touching your soft skin, or tasting the sweetness of your cunt on my tongue."

My breath hitches in my throat. "Oh, I'd like that. I don't feel very pretty lately. Just...pregnant."

"You are beautiful." His hand skims down to the rounded bulge of my belly, bigger than ever. "This is beautiful. And it fills me with fierce pride and joy to see you and know you are mine." He eases the other strap down, and my cleavage threatens to spill free. With a careful touch, Haeden brushes his knuckle over the valley of my breasts. "I love the changes in your body, and I like the belly because it is full of my kit. Do you know what I like best?"

"What?" I'm entranced by Haeden's seductive whispers.

"I love when you look over at me and smile, because you are happy with me and I with you."

That is so achingly sweet that I can't help but beam at him. I remember he has baggage of his own—that he resonated to someone before me who wanted nothing to do with him, and who died before they could fulfill resonance. Haeden almost died, too, and got a new cootie. I'm glad this one chose me, because I can't imagine my life without him. "You're making me feel a lot better about all the doubts I've had lately."

My big alien grins down at me. "That is my job. I am your mate. You have my heart. Why should we not talk about all of the things that bother us?"

"Because nothing bothers you!"

"It is because I am happy. I have my mate. I have two wonderful kits. My life is better than I have ever dreamed." He smiles, and then admits, "Though I would be happier if Joden slept in his own bed more often so I can mate with my female."

"That's my fault," I admit. I'm a noodle when it comes to the kids, and I suck at putting up boundaries. "I'll work on it with him. I want us to have our bed to ourselves, too."

"I like that idea. I also like how quiet it is with him visiting Suhmer and Warrek. You are clever, my mate. We should do this more often." He tugs at the bow between my breasts, pulling the knot free and then the leather falls about my belly, my breasts exposed to the air.

"I like that idea, too," I admit. Sleepovers are definitely the way to go.

"Your new tunic is interesting," he murmurs, gazing at my exposed breasts. "Is this why you were hiding away with Mah-dee for the last few days? You were making this impractical bit of leather?"

"Not everything has to be practical," I tell him, sliding my arms around his neck. "Maybe I just wanted you to look at me and say 'Damn, my mate is one sexy beast'."

"'Beast' is never a word I would use when thinking about my mate. Maybe 'soft' or 'fragile' or 'desirable.'"

"I like all those words better."

Haeden leans in and gives me another kiss, this one deeper and more intense than the last one. My hands curl against his neck and heat flutters low in my belly. Oh, god, a month is definitely far too long to wait between intense, toe-curling kisses that make me feel like liquid inside. He nips at my mouth, and then gently lowers me down to the furs.

I lie back against the pillows and furs, and as I do, he watches me with hungry eyes, devouring my half-naked body with a look. "Shall I show you all the parts that I find arousing on you, my Josee?"

"Go for it," I say, breathless.

My gorgeous Haeden leans over me and kisses me everywhere. He kisses my neck, my cheek, my ear, each milk-swollen breast, and the bump of my belly over and over again. "I love all of you," he tells me. "I love our kits. I love our family. I love that we resonate to each other, over and over, because it means we are meant to be."

My throat aches with love for this man. "I love you so much, Haeden. I don't know how I got so lucky as to have you in my life, but I'm so grateful you're mine."

"My beautiful Jo-see," he murmurs, and keeps kissing, moving lower. I moan when his hand nudges my knees apart in a familiar touch. It's his "I'm about to go down on you for hours" touch and it makes me positively *wet*. With a shuddering breath, I spread my legs. I can't see what's happening because his face is hidden— all I see are his horns rising above the crest of my belly.

And then he gives me a long, slow, forceful lick that drags over me from core to clit, and I come unglued. I whimper, twisting my hands in the furs as my gorgeous Haeden tongues me up and down, murmuring words of pleasure. He loves my taste, he tells me. He loves my scent. He loves the way my clit teases the tip of his tongue. He loves how hot I am and how soft my folds are and and and and…

And it seems like forever since I've come so hard, but I do, shuddering and brutal. My hips jerk against his mouth as he continues to lick me, whispering sweet words that barely register in my passion-glazed brain.

Then, he sits up, and I can see the fire in his eyes. He's hungry for more, my gloriously sexy mate, and when he moves to lie next to me, I roll onto my side. Pregnant sex usually involves the same positions over and over, but I don't mind, because it's still incredibly good sex. Haeden spoons me from behind, lifting one of my legs and then his cock presses into me. We mate side to side, his spur pressing against my backside with every stroke, and his fingers teasing my nipples as he nips at my neck and tells me how much he loves me.

I love his groan as he comes, love the flood of his hot release between my thighs. He'll bathe me tenderly later since I'm having trouble reaching that region, and I curl up against him, utterly content with the feel of his panting breath against my neck.

"You did not come again," he murmurs, his hand sliding between my thighs to rub against my clit. "Shall I help?"

"I'm in no rush," I say, closing my eyes and leaning back against him. I feel cuddled and loved and so, so good. My stupid lingerie is bunched around my waist and I probably look ridiculous, but I don't care. "We have all night. The slumber party was definitely a great idea."

"Mmm, we should have thought of it sooner." He nips at my shoulder, then presses a kiss there. "But do you know what we forgot?"

"What's that?"

"Tickling." His hand moves to my side, and then he's tickling me. I have to bite back my squeal so I don't wake Joha. Haeden's laughter brushes against my ears and I squirm against him. Turns out you can orgasm pretty quickly when your mate's cock is still inside you and you're being tickled.

I come so hard my brain feels as if it's a firecracker, and this time when I sag back against Haeden, I sigh with contentment. "That was not fair."

"No," he admits. "But it was enjoyable."

EPILOGUE

HAEDEN

I mate with my blushing Jo-see all night long. She naps while I hold her, and when she stirs between feedings, I let her nurse Joha and then claim her for myself all over again. By the time the dawn comes, she is yawning but goes to sleep with a smile on her face.

I trace her jaw gently, watching her as she sleeps. I am a fool, I decide. I am so busy trying to be a good father and a provider, setting extra traps and hunting twice as much to make up for the families with mates in the other village that I have forgotten that my Jo-see has a fragile heart and needs to be reminded that she is everything to me. Even though she smiles, she worries I will abandon her like everyone else in her past. It will never, ever do such a thing, but I am glad she spoke of her fears. After all, I am nothing if I do not have my Jo-see. Her love has saved me from my misery, and I vow I will do my best to never make her feel as if she is not wanted ever again.

It could not be further from the truth, after all.

So I let her sleep, and I wake her up a short time later by clutching at her buttocks, just as she demanded.

"Mm, what is it?" She blinks sleepy eyes at me.

"You wished to know when I needed you. I am showing you." I consider the feel of her backside against my hand and admit, "This is rather pleasurable."

Jo-see chuckles and wiggles against my hand, and I growl low in my throat. Does she wish to be taken again? But then Joha hiccups and begins to burble her nonsense sounds, indicating she is awake and the day must start.

We share a disappointed look.

I kiss my mate quickly. "You stay in bed. I will bring her to you."

Her eyes show her appreciation, and Joha nurses as I move around the hut, preparing for the day. When our daughter is done, she slides out of my mate's grip, toddling to my side with her arms open wide. "Pah-pah-pah!"

I love it when she says my name. I grab her and swing her into the air, her delighted shrieks filling the hut. "That is right! Pah-pah. And you are going to spend the day with Pah-pah, my little one."

"She is?" Jo-see fights back a yawn, sitting up in the bed. "You're taking her with you today?"

"I am. I will get Joden, too. We will go hunt some herbs to re-supply your tea stash, and check my traps. We will not go far." I pick up my daughter and immediately the smell of her wraps hits me. My lip curls. "But first, you must be changed, Joha."

"Pah-pah!" she shrieks happily.

It is a good thing I am only checking traps. When Joha is happy, she is almost as loud as Joden. I grin and roll out her changing mat, setting her down so I can put new clothes on my wriggling daughter. Once she is clean and changed, I dig out the harness I used for carrying Joden around until he grew too big, and strap it onto my chest and then slide my daughter into the pouch. Her little legs dangle from two leg-holes and she flails and kicks with excitement.

"Are you sure?" Jo-see asks, getting to her feet. She moves to my side and adjusts Joha's clothing, then puts protective fur boot-wraps over my daughter's legs to cover from the cold. "Both kits can be a handful."

"I am sure," I tell her, and lean forward for a kiss. "You get some rest. We will be up late tonight."

"Oh?"

My eyes gleam with promise. "Tickling."

She giggles, and then Joha giggles too, and the hut is filled with happiness.

♥

Suh-mer is thrilled when I arrive to retrieve Joden. Her eyes light up and she helps him dress quickly, even as Warrek looks on with amusement.

"My mate is not quite ready to be a mother to three energetic boys," he admits, looking fondly at Suh-mer.

"Joden is enough for anyone, much less two other boys." I move to my son's side and help him put on his boots, and then take his hand. "Come. We are going hunting."

"Yay!" he screams, and poor Suh-mer winces. We will have to

think of others that will watch our son for us, because I intend on having alone time with my Jo-see regularly once more. I did not realize how badly she needed it.

Joden is full of energy as he races down the path toward the lift. He chatters non-stop, telling me about his evening and how he and Masan and Rollan roasted seeds and stayed up late telling stories with Suh-mer and Warrek. He tells me how Masan has a pet dirtbeak and he has taught it to fetch things and to come when he calls it. I do not know if that is true, but my son is impressed. He continues to talk and talk and talk as we go up the lift and then head out on the trails. I can see the crusted footsteps of others who have come down this path earlier this morning, and watch as Joden bounces from footprint to footprint.

"Pah-pah!" Joha says, reaching up to pat my chin happily. "Pah-pah!"

"That's right," I tell her, smiling. She smiles back up at me, revealing one little tooth on her bottom gums, and my heart clenches because that smile is Jo-see's smile. I look up at my son, who is racing ahead. "Joden, come here."

"I'm checking the traps, Papa!" he calls.

I point at the spot beside me. "Come."

He makes a frustrated sound and stomps back to my side, all childish frustration. "But I want to see what we caught!"

"And we will. But first we must talk about important hunter things."

That gets his attention. He comes to my side, open curiosity in his eyes. "What sorts of hunter things?"

I take his gloved hand in mine and we walk. "You need to be careful of the things you say to Mama. She worries a lot about you and the kits. Both your sister Joha and the kit in her belly. It makes her anxious."

"Anxious like Miss Ariana?"

I clear my throat, because my mate's worries are not quite the same as Zolaya's fragile mate. "In a different way."

"Why is she anxious?"

"She worries she is not enough for us. That we are not happy."

"You haven't tickled Mommy lately," he tells me. "Does that mean you're not happy?"

I decide to be tactful. "Mama and I tickle, but we are just very quiet about it. And you should not be listening in. It is adult time when we are behind our screen and in the furs. Do you understand?"

He looks up at me with solemn eyes. "I heard Maddie and Hassen tickling yesterday and they weren't even in their furs."

I grunt and make a mental note to talk to Hassen. "Your mama and I are much quieter than them. But we are still happy." I squeeze his hand. "There is nothing that brings me more joy than your mother. Without her, I am but half a hunter. Do you understand? I need your mother like I need breath in my lungs."

Joden nods. "Mommy is special."

I smile down at him. "Very, very special."

"I think she's the best mommy in the village," he says, his voice dropping to a whisper.

"I think so, too, but we should keep that a secret between us." I put a finger to my lips, and Joha immediately reaches for my hand. I give her one of my braids instead, so she can tug on it to her heart's content.

Joden likes the idea of a secret. He is full of smiles, his little tail flicking back and forth. He is pleased with the knowledge that he has the best mother, and I can practically see his young mind weighing whether or not he should announce such a thing to the others. After a long pause, he looks up at me again. "What herbs are we hunting today? The ones with the red flowers from last time?"

I am surprised that my son remembered. "You are getting to be a big hunter if you can recall such things, Joden. I am pleased." He beams up at me, and I think of our problem with Joden crawling into bed with us every night. "Did you wet the bed last night at Suh-mer and Warrek's hut?"

"Nope!" He looks pleased with himself.

Mmm. That is interesting. I wonder if he does it so he has an excuse to sleep with us. I will have to tell Jo-see about this. "That is very good," I tell him, and an idea occurs to me. "You have grown into a strong hunter. Perhaps...perhaps it is time that you have a hunter's bed instead of a kit's bed."

His eyes go wide. "So I can be a hunter?"

"So you can train to be one," I correct. He is still little, my son, no matter how much he wants to grow up quickly. "If we make you a big hunter bed, will you sleep in it? That means you cannot sleep with Mommy and Papa. Big hunters do not do such things."

Joden is beside himself with excitement. "I want a big hunter bed!"

"Good." I am very pleased at this turn of events. "Very good."

MADDIE

I snuggle happily against my big barbarian's wide chest and give a sigh of pure pleasure. That was an amazing night, and one I'm not going to forget any time soon. "We should probably get up. It's morning."

"Mmm." Hassen caresses my butt. "I think I have fur stuck to my tail."

I giggle. The hraku syrup I made was fun, but the aftermath is... sticky. We've been sticking to the blankets all night long, not that it's really slowed us down much. I pull a white tuft of fur off of Hassen's blue hip. "It's definitely everywhere. I guess I'll have to wash all these furs."

"And wash your mate. Again." He grins and then pats my butt once more. "But for now, I should towel off quickly and go get our son. I promised I would spend the day with him."

I nod. "And then you'll be back? You're not going out again for a while, are you?" It's the nature of this tribe of hunter-gatherers that the men inevitably have to take long hunting trips. Before I was pregnant, I used to go with him, and we've talked about going all three of us when Masan is old enough. I guess that's another reason to not be ready for another baby. I kinda like the thought of the three of us doing stuff. Just...not yet. "I need you home for a while before you go venturing off again."

"I will be back," he tells me firmly, massaging my ample butt.

I'm about to suggest we do one more round before he heads out when a horrible squawking noise makes us both jump.

"What was that?" Hassen asks, astonished.

I sigh. "That would be Millicent, the dirtbeak."

Sure enough, a moment later there's a scratch at the door. I barely manage to pull the furs over our nudity before I see a flash of Warrek's long fluttering hair. Then, Masan charges in, his bird perched atop his hair. "Mama! Papa! I taught Millicent how to sit on my head!"

"Yay." I try to sound enthusiastic, but I just remember birds that liked to shit everywhere. Millicent looks happy, though. She's roosting, her claws curled in Masan's thick dark hair, and she flutters her feathers and settles down between his horns.

Hassen just looks shocked. He glances down at me again. "A...dirtbeak?"

"I know it's not ideal," I whisper. "But he loves the damn thing. If it gets to be a problem, we'll set it free."

Hassen only grins and wraps one of the furs around his loins, getting to his feet. "Show me your pet, my son." I reach up and un-stick the pelt from his butt cheek as he walks away, and then watch, brimming with pride, as my son and mate fuss over the stupid bird.

I'm so glad he's home. It hits me now, after a night of hardcore "reuniting" just how much I've missed my mate, my Hassen, my other half. I love him so much. I even love that he's thrilled with Masan and his bird. He laughs with delight as Masan shows how he's taught Millicent to come when he snaps his fingers. Sure enough, the bird flutters from the top of his head onto his shoulder, and pecks at his cheek. He gives her a seed, then beams at his father for approval.

"Very smart," Hassen says. "You know that K'thar of the island tribe has a pet flyer? It was a very ugly, fat little creature. Your Mill-sent is much better."

"I know, she's smart," Masan beams.

"Come, my son," Hassen says. "You and I are going to get dressed and then we are going to see about making Mill-sent a hut of her own that can sit near your furs. Would you like that?"

"Oh, yes."

"Give Mama a kiss and then let us go."

Hassen dresses quickly and Masan comes and showers me with kisses and tells me about his day while I lounge in bed, hiding my nudity with the furs. I smile at my sweet son, loving the excitement in his baby face as he talks. He needs his father home, too, I realize. Maybe we'll go on that family hunting trip the moment the bitter season returns.

I like that thought a lot.

"Let us let your mother rest," Hassen says, and winks at me as he takes Masan—and Millicent—with him.

I wave goodbye and blow kisses, and then it's just me, lying in very sticky furs and debating whether or not to go back to sleep. Last night was amazing…but tonight should be amazing, too. I'll definitely need some sleep, and a bath.

But first…

I get dressed quickly, trying to ignore how my clothes stick to my skin in places, and pull my hair back into a knot. Wrapping a heavy cloak around me, I head out of my hut and cross the long path that winds through the village, heading toward Josie and Haeden's hut. The screen's over the door, so I knock-scratch.

"Coming," Josie calls, and a moment later she appears, wrapped up in furs. She looks sleep-tousled, but when she sees me, she smiles widely. "Hey, Maddie."

"I'm not staying," I tell her quickly, and I grin. "I just wanted to see how your Valentine lingerie went over."

"He had no idea what it was about," she confesses. "But he got the gist of it soon enough. How was your Valentine's Day?"

"Fucking awesome." I give her a sly look. "How was yours?"

"Equally awesome…with an equal amount of fucking." Josie giggles.

And we share a fist bump.

AUTHOR'S NOTE

Ho, as the sa-khui say. Or just 'hey!' Or whatever. I never know how to start my author notes. Maybe I'll take a page from General Kenobi and say "Hello there!"

(That's a little Star Wars nerd humor for you.)

I'm asked a few things over on Facebook on a regular basis. One is usually where I'm asked to write more of the original tribe. That's usually followed by OMG PLEASE MORE HAEDEN AND JOSIE. Which is then followed by OMG MORE MADDIE AND HASSEN.

Okay, FINE. You WIN.

(I'm giggling. Those are two of my favorite couples, so this is not a chore to do. Like, at ALL.)

In all seriousness, I loved writing this little novella. It allowed me to go back to the 'old tribe' and visit, and give a little insight on the daily life. There's no big drama, mostly because I love seeing happy anecdotes more than anything else. Is it low key? Yes. Does it make me happy as fuck? Also yes.

So we have Maddie and Hassen reuniting - I really love this pair because he's completely gaga for her, and she loves asserting her femininity. She doesn't care that she's a bit of a freak. She owns it. I wish I was half as confident as she is! Their part of the story was nothing but pure rompy fun.

Josie's part is a little more 'less' fun and more sweet. She's one of those people that has a lot of history and while she doesn't let it bog her down, in weak moments, it can creep in and worry her. She needs to be reminded that she is loved and adored, but luckily Haeden is all too happy to take on that role. I love writing them, even if it's just the kind of 'reunion' that most busy parents have to squeeze in every now and then.

And speaking of reunions, I almost called this story Barbarian's Reunion because I thought it fit, but there were so many votes for Barbarian's Valentine as the title that I couldn't refuse. Plus, Kati made this cute cover that actually mirrors Josie and Haeden's initial cover. It's almost like we did that on purpose!

As for who is next — in THIS series, it will be BARBARIAN'S SEDUCTION and you bet I'm going to write Marlene and Zennek's initial get together and how she got all slinky and sexy with our blushing, shy Zennek. That one is going to be So. Stinking. Fun.

HOWEVER. I don't know if it's next next? There's a lot of lobbying on Facebook for N'dek over in the island tribe to get his heroine. And you know me, I listen to my fans! So once I get this contracted project off my desk (which will eat up the rest of my February), in March, I'll either be writing N'dek and his mystery heroine, or man-eater Marlene.

I've also said that I want to write more Ice Planet Barbarians (the original tribe!) this year, and I mean it. Once Marlene's book is written, I want to go back and write a full length story for

Megan/Cashol and Nora/Dagesh, both of whom got short stories only. So definitely more barbarian goodness on the way.

Someone actually asked me today if I was sick of writing my ice planet series.

Nope. I love it. I'm constantly thinking about the characters and dreaming up new scenarios. As long as you guys are still reading, I'll keep writing. <3

Much love <3

Ruby

PS - A small shout-out to the immersive IPB wiki run by Hannah. If you haven't seen this, she's done a TON of work and I love it! Thank you so much, Hannah!!!

PPS - I'm also on Instagram! I mostly post derpy stuff (and show off my lack of social media polish) and screenshots of word count. If you like Instagram, feel free to follow me. I can't promise EXCITING content but I'll try to add a little flavor to your feed. :)

PPPS - I really wanted to include an updated 'Cast of Characters' but Amazon's getting weird about what it considers 'bonus' content and this book might be too short to include something so lengthy. I'll have it in the next full length book, I promise!

CAST OF CHARACTERS

At Croatoan

Mated Couples and their kits

Vektal (Vehk-tall) – The chief of the sa-khui. Mated to Georgie.

Georgie – Human woman (and unofficial leader of the human females). Has taken on a dual-leadership role with her mate. Currently pregnant with her third kit.

Talie (Tah-lee) – Their first daughter.

Vekka (Veh-kah) – Their second daughter.

Maylak (May-lack) – Tribe healer. Mated to Kashrem.

Kashrem (Cash-rehm) - Her mate, also a leather-worker.

Esha (Esh-uh) – Their teenage daughter.

Makash (Muh-cash) — Their younger son.

Sevvah (Sev-uh) – Tribe elder, mother to Aehako, Rokan, and Sessah

Oshen (Aw-shen) – Tribe elder, her mate

Sessah (Ses-uh) - Their youngest son (currently at Icehome beach)

Ereven (Air-uh-ven) Hunter, mated to Claire.

Claire – Mated to Ereven

Erevair (Air-uh-vair) - Their first child, a son

Relvi (Rell-vee) – Their second child, a daughter

Liz – Raahosh's mate and huntress. Currently at Icehome beach.

Raahosh (Rah-hosh) – Her mate. A hunter and brother to Rukh. Currently at Icehome beach.

Raashel (Rah-shel) – Their daughter.

Aayla (Ay-lah) – Their second daughter

Ahsoka (Ah-so-kah) - Their third daughter.

Stacy – Mated to Pashov. Unofficial tribe cook.

Pashov (Pah-showv) – son of Kemli and Borran, brother to Farli, Zennek, and Salukh. Mate of Stacy. Currently at Icehome beach.

Pacy (Pay-see) – Their first son.

Tash (Tash) – Their second son.

―――

Nora – Mate to Dagesh. Currently pregnant after a second resonance.

Dagesh (Dah-zhesh) (the g sound is swallowed) – Her mate. A hunter.

Anna & Elsa – Their twin daughters.

―――

Harlow – Mate to Rukh. Once 'mechanic' to the Elders' Cave. Currently at Icehome beach.

Rukh (Rookh) – Former exile and loner. Original name Maarukh. (Mah-rookh). Brother to Raahosh. Mate to Harlow. Father to Rukhar. Currently at Icehome beach.

Rukhar (Roo-car) – Their son.

Daya (dye-uh) - Their daughter.

―――

Megan – Mate to Cashol. Mother to Holvek. Pregnant.

Cashol (Cash-awl) – Mate to Megan. Hunter. Father to Holvek.

Holvek (Haul-vehk) – their son.

―――

Marlene (Mar-lenn) – Human mate to Zennek. French.

Zennek (Zehn-eck) – Mate to Marlene. Father to Zalene. Brother to Pashov, Salukh, and Farli. Currently at Icehome beach.

Zalene (Zah-lenn) – daughter to Marlene and Zennek.

―――

Ariana – Human female. Mate to Zolaya. Basic school 'teacher' to tribal kits.

Zolaya (Zoh-lay-uh) – Hunter and mate to Ariana. Father to Analay & Zoari.

Analay (Ah-nuh-lay) – Their son.

Zoari (Zoh-air-ee) - Their newborn daughter.

Tiffany – Human female. Mated to Salukh. Tribal botanist.

Salukh (Sah-luke) – Hunter. Son of Kemli and Borran, brother to Farli, Zennek, and Pashov. Currently at Icehome beach.

Lukti (Lookh-tee) – Their son.

Aehako (Eye-ha-koh) –Mate to Kira, father to Kae. Son of Sevvah and Oshen, brother to Rokan and Sessah.

Kira – Human woman, mate to Aehako, mother of Kae. Was the first to be abducted by aliens and wore an ear-translator for a long time. Recently re-resonated to her mate a 2nd time.

Kae (Ki –rhymes with 'fly') – Their daughter.

Kemli (Kemm-lee) – Female elder, mother to Salukh, Pashov, Zennek, and Farli. Tribe herbalist.

Borran (Bore-awn) – Her mate, elder. Tribe brewer.

Josie – Human woman. Mated to Haeden. Currently pregnant for a third time.

Haeden (Hi-den) – Hunter. Previously resonated to Zalah, but she died (along with his khui) in the khui-sickness before resonance could be completed. Now mated to Josie.

Joden (Joe-den) – Their first child, a son.

Joha (Joe-hah) – Their second child, a daughter.

Rokan (Row-can) – Oldest son to Sevvah and Oshen. Brother to Aehako and Sessah. Adult male hunter. Now mated to Lila. Has 'sixth' sense.

Lila – Maddie's sister. Once hearing impaired, recently reacquired on *The Tranquil Lady* via med bay. Resonated to Rokan.

Rollan (Row-lun) – Their first child, a son.

Lola (nicknamed Lolo) - Their recently born daughter.

Hassen (Hass-en) – Hunter. Previously exiled. Mated to Maddie. Currently at Icehome beach.

Maddie – Lila's sister. Found in second crash. Mated to Hassen.

Masan (Mah-senn) – Their son.

Asha (Ah-shuh) – Mate to Hemalo. Mother to Hashala (deceased) and Shema.

Hemalo (Hee-muh-low) – Mate to Asha. Father to Hashala (deceased) and Shema.

Shema (Shee-muh) – Their daughter.

Farli – (Far-lee) Adult daughter to Kemli and Borran. Her brothers are Salukh, Zennek, and Pashov. She has a pet dvisti named Chompy (Chahm-pee). Mated to Mardok. Pregnant. Currently at Icehome beach.

Mardok (Marr-dock) – Bron Mardok Vendasi, from the planet Ubeduc VII. Arrived on *The Tranquil Lady*. Mechanic and ex-soldier. Resonated to Farli and elected to stay behind with the tribe. Currently at Icehome beach.

———

Bek – (Behk) – Hunter. Brother to Maylak. Mated to Elly.

Elly – Former human slave. Kidnapped at a very young age and has spent much of life in a cage or enslaved. First to resonate amongst the former slaves brought to Not-Hoth. Mated to Bek. Pregnant.

———

Harrec (Hair-ek) – Hunter. Squeamish. Also a tease. Recently resonated to Kate.

Kate – Human female. Extremely tall & strong, with white-blonde curly hair. Recently resonated to Harrec. Pregnant.

Mr. Fluffypuff aka Puff/Poof - Her orphaned snowcat kitten.

———

Warrek (War-ehk) – Tribal hunter and teacher. Son to Eklan (now deceased). Resonated to Summer.

Summer – Human female. Tends to ramble in speech when nervous. Chess aficionado. Recently resonated to Warrek.

———

Taushen (Tow – rhymes with cow – shen) – Hunter. Recently mated to Brooke. Experiencing a happiness renaissance. Currently at Icehome beach.

Brooke – Human female with fading pink hair. Former hairdresser, fond of braiding the hair of anyone that walks close enough. Mated to Taushen and recently pregnant. Currently at Icehome beach.

=====

Vaza (Vaw-zhuh) – Widower and elder. Loves to creep on the ladies. Currently pleasure-mated with Gail and at Icehome beach. Adopted father to Z'hren.

Gail – Divorced older human woman. Had a son back on Earth (deceased). Approx fiftyish in age. Pleasure-mated with Vaza, adopted mother to Z'hren.

Unmated Elders

=====

Drayan (Dry-ann) – Elder.

Drenol (Dree-nowl) – Elder. Friend to Luke.

Vadren (Vaw-dren) – Elder.

IPB READING LIST

ICE PLANET BARBARIANS

Ice Planet Barbarians

Barbarian Alien

Barbarian Lover

Barbarian Mine

Ice Planet Holiday (novella)

Barbarian's Prize

Barbarian's Mate

Having the Barbarian's Baby (short story)

Ice Ice Babies (short story)

Barbarian's Touch

Calm (short story)

Barbarian's Taming

Aftershocks (short story)

Barbarian's Heart

Barbarian's Hope

Barbarian's Choice

Barbarian's Redemption

Barbarian's Lady

Barbarian's Rescue

Barbarian's Tease

The Barbarian Before Christmas (novella)

Barbarian's Beloved

THE ICEHOME SERIES

LAUREN'S BARBARIAN

A lush, tropical island on an icy planet makes no sense. Then again, not much makes sense anymore after waking up and finding myself on a strange world populated by aliens. Here, I no longer need my glasses to see…which is good, because I'm far too busy staring at a sexy, four-armed alien named K'thar…

VERONICA'S DRAGON

Everyone expects resonance to happen when twenty newcomers are dropped onto the frosty world...and no one expects the gorgeous, golden god named Ashtar to resonate to someone like me, though. He's fierce. Flirty. Powerful. Disgustingly handsome. I'm...not any of those things.

But resonance seems to think we'd be great together. And Ashtar does, too...

WILLA'S BEAST

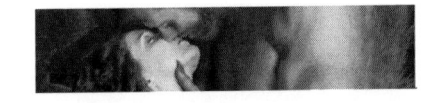

Beast. Creature. Monster.
Dangerous.
All of these things have been said about Gren.
Willa doesn't mind that he's a beast, as long as he's *her* beast.

GAIL'S FAMILY

Gail's happy with Vaza, her new world, and her life on the ice planet. But when a chance to become a mom once more arises... will she change her world once more?
(A novella)

ANGIE'S GLADIATOR

She's pregnant with a baby...and she doesn't know who or *what* the father is. He's a clone and a gladiator, and he doesn't care about Angie's past. All he knows is that he's never wanted anything as much as he's wanted the fragile human female...

WANT MORE?

For more information about upcoming books in the Ice Planet Barbarians, Fireblood Dragons, or any other books by Ruby Dixon, like me on Facebook or subscribe to my new release newsletter. I love sharing snippets of books in progress and fan art! Come join the fun.

As always - thanks for reading!

<3 Ruby

PS - Want to discuss my books without me staring over your shoulder? There's a group for that, too! Ruby Dixon - Blue Barbarian Babes (over on Facebook) has all of your barbarian and dragon needs. :) Enjoy!

PPS - I'm now on Instagram!

ALSO BY RUBY DIXON

FIREBLOOD DRAGONS

Fire in His Blood

Fire in His Kiss

Fire in His Embrace

Fire in His Fury

Fire In His Spirit

Fire in His Veins

CORSAIRS

THE CORSAIR'S CAPTIVE

IN THE CORSAIR'S BED

ENTICED BY THE CORSAIR

DECEIVING THE CORSAIR

STAND ALONE

PRISON PLANET BARBARIAN

THE ALIEN'S MAIL-ORDER BRIDE

BEAUTY IN AUTUMN

THE KING'S SPINSTER BRIDE

THE ALIEN ASSASSIN'S CONVENIENT WIFE

BEDLAM BUTCHERS

Bedlam Butchers, Volumes 1-3: Off Limits, Packing Double, Double Trouble

Bedlam Butchers, Volumes 4-6: Double Down, Double or Nothing, Slow Ride

Double Dare You

BEAR BITES

SHIFT: Five Complete Novellas

Made in the USA
Middletown, DE
14 April 2022